CARTER HIGH
M Y S T E R I E S

AZTEC RING

Mystery

By Eleanor Robins

D0869454

SADDLEBACK
EDUCATIONAL PUBLISHING

CARTER HIGH®
M Y S T E R I E S

SADDLEBACK
EDUCATIONAL PUBLISHING
www.sdlback.com

Copyright ©2006, 2011 by Saddleback Educational Publishing

ISBN-13: 978-1-61651-561-4
ISBN-10: 1-61651-561-9
eBook: 978-1-61247-129-7

Printed in Malaysia

20 19 18 17 16   6 7 8 9 10

Chapter 1

Jack sat at the bus stop. His friends Drake, Logan, and Lin were there, too.

Jack said, "Don't forget our science class is in the science lab today."

Jack had Mr. Zane for science. Logan and Drake had Mr. Zane for science, too. But they weren't in Jack's class.

"Why are we meeting in the lab?" Logan asked.

"Mr. Flint is coming today. And he needs a big room for his exhibit," Jack said.

"Oh, yeah. I forgot he's coming today," Logan said.

"I wish I could see the exhibit," Lin said.

But Lin didn't have Mr. Zane for science.

Mr. Flint was going to bring some necklaces, vases, and his Aztec ring.

He would stay all day. All of Mr. Zane's students would get to see his exhibit.

"This will be a good day," Logan said.

"That's for sure," Jack said.

"Not for me. I have a history test," Drake said.

"I have a test, too. But we'll have an easy day in science. We'll get to see the exhibit. And we won't have to work in class," Logan said.

"And Mr. Flint will bring his Aztec ring. That's the best of all," Jack said.

"Yeah," said Drake. "I read about the Aztec ring in the paper. It's worth a lot of money."

"For sure," Jack said.

"I wonder why Mr. Flint wants to bring the ring to school. He might lose it," Lin said.

"Yeah, or someone might steal it," Logan said.

"No one will steal the ring, Logan," Lin said.

"That's for sure," Jack said.

"Don't be too sure about that, Jack," Drake said.

Jack thought Logan and Drake were joking. But he wasn't so sure they were.

"Mr. Zane said we can't touch the exhibit. Not one thing," Jack said.

So how could someone steal the Aztec ring?

Lin said, "I don't think someone would steal the ring. But it's worth a lot of money. And I still wonder why Mr. Flint would bring it to school."

"He wants to show the ring to us. That's why he's bringing it to school," Jack said.

Jack could hardly wait to see the Aztec ring.

That was for sure.

Chapter 2

Jack was on his way to his science class. He was in a hurry to get there. Some students had seen the exhibit. They said it was really great.

Jack hurried into the science lab. He wanted to get a good seat. So he sat in the front row.

The bell rang.

Mr. Zane called the roll.

Then he said, "Mr. Flint is here today. He's going to show you his exhibit now. And he's going to tell you about it."

Mr. Zane went over to a chair and sat down.

Mr. Flint smiled at the students. He said, "I'm glad to be here today. It took me a long time to find all of these things. All of them mean a lot to me. And I'm glad to show them to you."

"And we're glad you're here, Mr. Flint," Jack said.

That was for sure.

Mr. Flint looked at Jack. "Thank you," he said.

Mr. Flint started to tell the class about his exhibit. And he told them how he found all of his things.

Then Mr. Flint went over to a table. The table was away from the other tables. The Aztec ring was on this table. He picked up the ring.

Mr. Flint said, "I'll walk around the room. And I'll show you my Aztec ring. Then you can get up. And you can look at my other things."

Mr. Flint started to walk around the room. He had the ring in his hand. He walked up one row. He showed it to those students.

Then he walked up Jack's row.

One boy said, "That's some ring. It must be worth a lot of money."

"Yes. It's worth lot of money," Mr. Flint said.

"I wish I had a ring like that. That's for sure," Jack said.

Mr. Flint looked at Jack. He said, "I'm sure you do, young man. I'm sure you do."

Then Mr. Flint laughed.

He showed the ring to the other students in the class. Then he put it back on the table.

Mr. Zane stood up.

Mr. Zane said, "Thank you so much for coming today, Mr. Flint. I know my students are very glad you're here."

"Thank you. And I'm very glad to be here," Mr. Flint said.

Mr. Zane looked at the students. He said, "Now you can get up. You can look at the exhibit. Then you can go to lunch. But don't touch anything. Not even one thing."

Mr. Zane had told them that rule many times before Mr. Flint came.

"And stay away from the ring," Mr. Zane said.

Jack quickly got up. He walked over to the exhibit. He looked at the necklaces first. Then he looked at the vases. But he didn't touch any of them.

Most of the students wanted to go to lunch early. So they quickly looked at the exhibit.

Jack wasn't in a hurry. So he looked at the exhibit slowly.

Jack wished he could look at the Aztec ring again. But he knew he had to stay away from it.

Chapter 3

It was lunchtime. But Jack was still looking at the exhibit.

Mr. Zane said, "Time for all of you to go to lunch. Mr. Flint has to eat lunch, too."

The other students hurried out of the lab. But Jack walked over to talk to Mr. Flint.

Jack said, "Thank you for coming, Mr. Flint. This is a great exhibit. And thank you for bringing the Aztec ring."

"I'm glad you like it, young man. I like it best of all my things. I guess you do, too," Mr. Flint said.

"For sure," Jack said.

Only Jack and Mr. Flint were still in the room. Mr. Zane had gone out into the hall.

Mr. Flint said, "Would you like to look at the ring again?"

That surprised Jack very much.

"Yes. Is it okay for me to do that?" Jack asked.

"Yes, young man. It's my ring. And I trust you. You can pick it up. So you can see it better. Just be very careful with it. It's worth a lot of money," Mr. Flint said.

"But you need to go to lunch, Mr. Flint" Jack said.

Mr. Flint said, "I'm glad you like my ring. I can wait to go to lunch. I don't mind doing that. So go over and look at my ring."

Jack wasn't sure he should do that. Mr. Zane had said to stay away from the ring. But Jack wanted to see the ring again. And Mr. Flint said he could look at it. And he could pick it up.

Jack knew he shouldn't go over to the ring. But he did.

Mr. Flint went out to the hall. Mr. Zane was still in the hall. Jack could hear Mr. Flint talking to Mr. Zane.

Jack wanted to pick up the ring. He knew he shouldn't do that. But Mr. Flint said it was okay to pick up the ring. So he did.

Jack looked at the door. Mr. Flint stood in the doorway. He was looking at Jack.

Jack looked at the ring for a few minutes. Then he put it on the table.

Then Jack went out to the hall.

Jack said, "That's a great ring, Mr. Flint. Thank you for saying I could look at it again."

Mr. Zane walked over to them. He seemed surprised to see Jack.

He said, "I didn't know you were still in the science lab, Jack. I thought you'd gone to lunch."

Mr. Zane didn't seem pleased.

Mr. Flint said, "How did you like all of my things, young man?"

"They're great," Jack said.

Jack didn't know why Mr. Flint asked him that. He'd already told Mr. Flint how much he liked the exhibit.

"How did you like my ring?" Mr. Flint asked.

"The best of all," Jack said.

But why did Mr. Flint ask him that?

Mr. Flint already knew he liked the ring best of all.

Mr. Zane said, "I hope you didn't touch anything, Jack. And I hope you didn't touch that ring."

Mr. Flint spoke before Jack could answer him.

Mr. Flint said, "This young man needs to go to lunch. So we need to let him get on his way. We don't want him to be late."

Mr. Flint seemed in a hurry for Jack to go. But he knew that Jack needed to go to lunch.

Mr. Flint went into the science lab.

Jack walked down the hall.

He looked back. Mr. Zane was still in the hall. He was looking at Jack. He didn't seem pleased.

Then Mr. Flint ran out of the room. He was yelling. He said, "Stop that young man. Stop that young man. He took my Aztec ring."

Did someone take the Aztec ring?

And who was the young man Mr. Flint was yelling about?

Mr. Flint ran down the hall. He had one hand on his coat pocket. He was pointing at Jack with his other hand.

Did he think Jack took the ring?

Chapter 4

Mr. Zane ran down the hall, too. And he yelled. "Jack, come back here. Come back here," he yelled.

Mr. Zane seemed very upset.

Did they think Jack took the ring? But it was in the lab. Why didn't Mr. Flint see it?

Jack quickly walked back to Mr. Zane and Mr. Flint. They stopped running down the hall. And they waited for Jack.

"What's wrong?" Jack asked.

"That's what I want to know," Mr. Zane said.

Mr. Flint said, "You took my ring. And you must give it back."

"I didn't take your ring. Your ring is still in the science lab," Jack said.

Mr. Flint said, "No. It isn't in the lab. You took my ring. And you need to give it back to me."

Mr. Zane seemed very upset. But Mr. Flint didn't seem that upset.

Mr. Flint put his hand on his pocket again. And Jack wondered why. Mr. Flint didn't do that when he talked to the class. Was that a sign Mr. Flint wasn't feeling well?

Some students walked by slowly. The students looked at the three of them talking.

Mr. Zane said, "We need to go into the lab. We shouldn't talk about this in the hall."

"I think we should go into the lab, too.

The ring's still there. You can both see it," Jack said.

Jack didn't take the ring. He left it in the lab. So it had to be in the lab. Where else could it be?

The three hurried into the lab.

They quickly walked over to the table. Jack had left the Aztec ring on that table. But the ring wasn't there.

Jack couldn't believe it was gone. How could it be gone?

Mr. Flint pointed to the table. He said, "See. The ring is gone. And this young man took it."

Mr. Zane looked at Jack. He asked, "Why were you in the lab by yourself, Jack? You shouldn't have been in here alone. I thought you had gone to lunch."

Jack said, "Mr. Flint said I could stay. And he told me that I could look at the Aztec ring."

Mr. Zane looked at Mr. Flint.

He asked, "Did you tell Jack he could stay and look at the Aztec ring?"

"Yes. But I thought I could trust the young man. I didn't think he would take the ring," Mr. Flint said.

Mr. Flint had his hand on his pocket again. Had the missing ring made him feel sick?

"I didn't take the ring. It was here when I left," Jack said.

"I don't want to believe you took the ring, young man. But you were the only one in here. I came in right after you left. And no one else came in," Mr. Flint said.

"But I didn't take the ring. It was on the table when I left. That's for sure," Jack said.

Mr. Zane said, "I don't want to think you took the ring, Jack. But the ring is gone. And no one else could've taken it."

Mr. Flint said, "Just give me the ring back, young man. I don't want to get you in any trouble. So I won't press any charges."

"But I don't have the Aztec ring," Jack said.

Why didn't they believe him?

"Maybe it fell onto the floor," Jack said.

Jack looked under the table. But he didn't see the ring.

"Maybe it fell onto the floor. And then it rolled under something else," Jack said.

Jack looked under everything in the lab. But he didn't see the ring.

Mr. Flint said, "Don't waste our time, young man. My ring didn't fall onto the floor. You took it. And you need to give it back to me."

"But I don't have it. I didn't take it," Jack said again.

Mr. Zane said, "This is a matter for Mr. Glenn."

Mr. Glenn was the principal.

"I'll lock this door. And we'll go to his office," Mr. Zane said.

Mr. Flint said, "Just give me the ring, young man. And we won't have to talk to the principal about this."

"But I don't have the Aztec ring," Jack said.

Why didn't they believe him?

Mr. Zane said, "Then I don't have a choice, Jack. We have to go and talk to Mr. Glenn."

Mr. Zane quickly locked the room. And the three of them walked to Mr. Glenn's office.

Chapter 5

The three got to Mr. Glenn's office. They went into the office. Jack had never been in his office before.

Mr. Zane told Mr. Glenn the Aztec ring was missing. And he said Mr. Flint thought Jack took it.

Mr. Glenn said, "I know you need to be at lunch, Mr. Zane. So you go on to lunch. And I'll talk to Mr. Flint and Jack about this."

Mr. Zane left.

Mr. Glenn closed the door. Then he sat down behind his desk. Jack and

Mr. Flint sat down in the two chairs in front of his desk.

Mr. Glenn said, "Now tell me all about this. You start, Mr. Flint."

Mr. Flint said, "I brought my Aztec ring to school. I wanted to show it to your students. I thought I could trust them. But this young man took my ring. And it's worth a lot of money."

"I can't believe one of my students took your ring," Mr. Glenn said.

"Well, one of them did. And it was this young man," Mr. Flint said.

"I didn't take it. I wouldn't do something like that," Jack said. Jack knew he sounded very upset. And he was very upset. Mr. Flint said, "Don't get upset, young man. I don't want to get you in any trouble. So I won't press charges. Just give me the ring back. And I'll forget you took it."

"I didn't take the ring. And I don't know where it is," Jack said.

Why didn't the man believe him?

Mr. Flint looked at Mr. Glenn.

He said, "I don't want to get this young man in trouble. So I won't press charges. But I must get my ring back."

"I didn't take the Aztec ring," Jack said again.

Mr. Flint looked at Jack.

He said, "But you were the only one in the room. No one else was in there. So you must have taken my ring. Who else could have?"

Jack didn't have an answer to that. But he did think of something.

He said, "You can look in my backpack. And you can look in my pockets."

Jack pulled his pockets inside out. The ring wasn't in them. Then he dumped his backpack on the floor. The ring wasn't in it either.

Mr. Glenn said, "Please wait outside, Mr. Flint. I want to talk to Jack by himself."

"Okay, but that young man took my Aztec ring. And I want it back," Mr. Flint said. Mr. Flint didn't sound mad. And he didn't seem mad. That surprised Jack.

Mr. Flint stood up. He had his hand on his pocket again. He walked to the door and opened it. He went out of the room. But he didn't close the door.

Mr. Glenn got up. He walked to the door and closed it. Then he sat down in the chair next to Jack.

Mr. Glenn said, "Jack, you heard what Mr. Flint said. He won't press any charges. He just wants his ring back. So you need to tell him where it is."

"I didn't take the ring. And I don't know where it is," Jack said.

28

Why didn't Mr. Glenn believe him?

Mr. Glenn said, "Then you tell me what happened, Jack."

"Class was over. Mr. Flint said I could stay. And he said I could look at the Aztec ring. So I did," Jack said.

"Where was Mr. Zane at this time?" Mr. Glenn asked.

"He was in the hall," Jack said.

"Where was Mr. Flint at this time?" Mr. Glenn asked.

"He went out to the hall. And he talked to Mr. Zane," Jack said.

"Who was in the science lab with you?" Mr. Glenn asked.

"No one," Jack said.

"So you were in there alone?" Mr. Glenn said.

"Yes," Jack said.

"Did you touch the ring?" Mr. Glenn asked.

"Yes," Jack said.

"Tell me the truth, Jack. Did you take the ring?" Mr. Glenn said.

"No. I didn't take the Aztec ring," Jack said. He was almost yelling at Mr. Glenn. But he didn't mean to yell.

Mr. Glenn said, "It's your lunchtime, Jack. You should be at lunch. So you can go now."

Jack was glad Mr. Glenn said he could leave. Jack could hardly wait to get out of Mr. Glenn's office.

Jack got up to go.

Mr. Glenn said, "Think about the ring, Jack. I'll talk to you again after lunch. And I hope we can get this worked out then. Mr. Flint doesn't want me to call the police. And I don't want to do that. But we have to find that ring. Or I must call the police."

Jack didn't know where the ring was. So he was sure Mr. Glenn would have to call the police.

Mr. Glenn and Mr. Zane didn't believe him. So he didn't think the police would either.

Jack opened the door and hurried out. Mr. Flint stood outside the door. But he didn't say anything to Jack.

Jack almost ran to the lunchroom. He needed to see his friends. He needed someone to help him. And he was sure they would try to do that.

But Jack wasn't sure how his friends could help him.

Chapter 6

Jack got to the lunchroom. He was late. He quickly got his lunch. Then he looked for his friends.

Drake waved to him. Drake was sitting with Logan, Paige, and Willow.

Paige and Willow lived at Grayson Apartments, too.

Jack hurried over to their table and sat down.

"Why are you late?" Paige asked.

"Did you hear the news? Some kid stole the Aztec ring," Drake said.

"You don't look so good, dude. Are you sick?" Logan asked.

Willow said, "One at a time. Give Jack a chance to answer."

Drake spoke first. He said, "Did you hear the news? Some guy stole the Aztec ring."

Jack said, "I'm that guy. But I didn't steal the Aztec ring."

The other four seemed very surprised to hear it.

"What do you mean you're that kid?" Drake asked.

Paige said, "You don't seem like you're joking, Jack. But you must be. You would never steal the ring."

Jack said, "That's for sure. I didn't steal the ring. But Mr. Flint said that I did. He said I was the only one who could have."

"No wonder you look sick, Jack," Logan said.

"We know you didn't steal it, Jack.

But why does Mr. Flint think you did?" Willow asked.

Jack told them he stayed after class to look at the ring. And he told them he was in the science lab by himself.

"Why did you stay in the lab by yourself? That was a dumb thing to do," Logan said.

"That wasn't nice, Logan," Willow said.

Logan said, "Maybe not. But it's true. And you should have known better, Jack."

"I know. But I wanted to see the ring," Jack said.

"We might have done the same thing," Paige said.

"Not me," Logan said.

"Or me," Drake said.

Willow said, "Don't make Jack feel worse. We need to talk about how to help him."

"Where was the ring when you left the

lab?" Paige asked.

"On the table," Jack said.

"Did someone come into the lab before you left?" Drake asked.

"No," Jack said.

"Where were Mr. Flint and Mr. Zane?" Logan asked.

"They were in the hall. Just outside the door," Jack said.

"They should know who went into the lab after you left. Maybe that person took it. Who was it?" Willow asked.

"Mr. Flint, that's who. And the ring was gone. But I don't know how. I didn't take it," Jack said.

"We know you didn't," Paige said.

"Yeah," said Logan. "That's one thing we know."

"Maybe the ring fell onto the floor. Did you look there?" Drake asked.

"Yes," Jack said.

"Maybe it fell onto the floor. And then it rolled under something, Jack," Paige said.

"I looked all over the lab. The ring wasn't in the lab," Jack said.

"That doesn't make much sense," Logan said.

"No, it doesn't," Willow said.

The five sat for a few minutes. And they didn't talk. But all five were thinking about the ring.

Then Jack said, "What am I going to do? How can I prove I didn't take the Aztec ring?"

Paige said, "Mr. Flint went into the lab after you left. And he was the only one to do that. And then he said the ring was gone. Is that right?"

"Yes, that's right," Jack said.

"So what about it?" Logan asked.

"Only one person could've taken the

ring," Paige said.

"Who?" the other four asked at the same time.

"Mr. Flint," Paige said.

Chapter 7

The other four seemed surprised by what Paige just said.

"But that can't be true," Jack said.

"That was a dumb thing to say, Paige. Why would Mr. Flint take the ring? It's his ring," Logan said.

"Yeah, Paige. Why would he take his own ring?" Drake asked.

"Maybe so he could keep the ring. And still get the insurance money," Paige said.

"We don't know he has insurance on the ring," Willow said.

"He must have it. The ring is worth a lot of money," Paige said.

"Mr. Flint took the ring. For sure," Jack said.

Logan said, "Okay, maybe Mr. Flint did take the ring. But what did he do with it?"

"That's what we have to find out," Paige said.

"And we don't have much time to do it," Willow said.

"You said Mr. Flint went into the lab. Then he quickly came out. And he said you took the ring. Right, Jack?" Paige asked.

"Yes," Jack said.

"Then he must have put it somewhere in the lab," Paige said.

"But where?" Drake asked.

"I looked all over the lab. The ring wasn't in there," Jack said.

"It has to be there," Paige said.

"Yeah," Drake said.

"But where?" Logan asked.

"I looked all over the lab. The ring wasn't in there," Jack said again.

"We have to think of where it could be. And fast. Lunchtime is almost over," Willow said.

The five didn't talk for a few minutes. They were trying to think of where the ring could be.

Then Willow asked, "How did Mr. Flint seem after he said the ring was gone?"

"Yeah, did he seem mad? Or upset?" Logan asked.

Jack said, "He didn't seem mad. But I think the missing ring made him feel sick."

"What do you mean?" Logan asked.

"Why do you think the missing ring made him sick, Jack?" Paige asked.

"Mr. Flint put his hand on his coat pocket. He did it many times. Like he didn't feel well," Jack said.

Paige got a big smile on her face. Paige said, "Or maybe the ring was in his pocket. And he didn't want it to fall out."

"Or he wanted to make sure the ring was still there," Drake said.

"I think you may be right, Paige. But how can we prove it?" Willow asked.

"Yes. How can we prove it, Paige?" Jack asked.

"We have to find a way to look in his coat pocket," Paige said.

"But how?" Jack asked.

Chapter 8

Jack saw Mr. Glenn come into the lunchroom. Jack was sure Mr. Glenn had come to see him. And he was right.

Mr. Glenn came over to Jack's table. He looked at Jack.

Mr. Glenn said, "I came to walk you to my office, Jack."

Willow said, "I'm glad you did, Mr. Glenn. We want to talk to you."

Willow told Mr. Glenn that they thought the Aztec ring was in Mr. Flint's coat pocket.

"It's hard to believe Mr. Flint took his own ring. But I know Jack. It's also very hard to believe you took it," Mr. Glenn said.

That made Jack feel a lot better.

Mr. Glenn said, "Come on, Jack. We'll go to the science lab. Maybe Mr. Flint is there. And I can find out the truth."

Jack and Mr. Glenn quickly left the lunchroom. They went to the science lab. Mr. Flint and Mr. Zane were there. Mr. Flint was packing up his exhibit.

Mr. Glenn asked, "What are you doing, Mr. Flint?"

But Jack knew Mr. Glenn could see what Mr. Flint was doing.

Mr. Flint said, "I can't trust the kids in your school. And I'm packing my things up. So I can take them home."

"I don't think you should do that," Mr. Glenn said.

Mr. Flint seemed very surprised. "Why?" he asked.

"The ring hasn't been found. And I'm

going to call the police. You'll need to be here to talk to them," Mr. Glenn said.

"I'll come back. After I take my things home. I need to get them away from your kids. I can't trust them," Mr. Flint said.

Then Mr. Flint put his hand on his pocket again.

"I'm sure the police will want you to stay here, Mr. Flint," Mr. Glenn said.

"Why? I said I'll come back," Mr. Flint said.

"Because Jack wasn't the only one alone in here with the ring. Someone else was alone in here with it, too," Mr. Glenn said.

Mr. Flint seemed very surprised. "Who?" he asked.

"You," Mr. Glenn said.

Jack spoke for the first time. He said, "The police might think the ring got into your things. Or that it fell off the table. Maybe the ring's in your pocket. And you don't know it's in there."

But Jack didn't believe that. He was sure Mr. Flint knew the Aztec ring was in there.

Mr. Flint seemed mad.

"That's a dumb idea. The ring isn't in my pocket," Mr. Flint said.

Mr. Glenn said, "It may not be, Mr. Flint. But maybe you should turn your pocket inside out. So you can make sure it isn't in there."

"I won't. How dare you say I took my own ring? That young man took it," Mr. Flint said.

Mr. Glenn said, "I didn't say you took it. But the police will want to make sure you don't have it. So I think they'll ask you to turn your pocket inside out."

"Maybe the ring is in your pocket. And you don't know it's in there," Jack said again.

Mr. Flint stood there for a few minutes. His face was very red. And he seemed very mad.

Then he put his hand into his coat pocket. And he pulled out the ring. "Well, what do you know?" he said. "Sorry about that, young man. My ring did fall into my pocket. And I didn't know it did."

Jack didn't believe Mr. Flint. And he didn't think Mr. Glenn did either. But he wasn't sure about that.

Mr. Glenn said, "I'm glad you found the ring, Mr. Flint. Now I think you should go. I'll watch you pack up your things. And then I'll walk you to your car."

Mr. Glenn looked at Jack. He said, "You don't need to stay here any longer, Jack. You can go to your next class."

Now Jack knew Mr. Glenn didn't believe Mr. Flint. For sure.

Dogs on wheels
Travelling with your canine companion

Norm Mort

Also from Veloce Publishing –
Buying your first motorcycle (Henshaw)
Caring for your bicycle – How to maintain and repair your bicycle (Henshaw)
Caring for your car – How to maintain and service your car (Fry)
Caring for your car's bodywork & interior (Nixon)
Caring for your scooter – How to maintain and service your 49cc to 125cc twist and go scooter (Fry)
Dogs on wheels – Travelling with your canine companion (Mort)
Electric cars – The future is now! (Linde)
First Aid for your car – Your expert guide to common problems and how to fix them (Collins)
How your car works – Your guide to the components & systems of modern cars, including hybrid and electrical vehicles (Linde)
How your motorcycle works – Your guide to the components & systems of modern motorcycles (Henshaw)
Land Rover Series I-III – Your expert guide to common problems and how to fix them (Thurman)
MG Midget & AH Sprite – Your expert guide to common problems and how to fix them (Thurman)
Motorcycles – A first-time buyer's guide (Henshaw)
Motorhomes – A first time buyer's guide (Fry)
Pass the MoT test! – How to check & prepare your car for the annual MoT test (Paxton)
Roads with a View – England's greatest views and how to find them by road (Corfield)
Roads with a View – Scotland's greatest views and how to find them by road (Corfield)
Roads with a View – Wales' greatest views and how to find them by road (Corfield)
Simple fixes for your car – How to do small jobs yourself and save money (Collins)
Selling your car – How to make your car look great and how to sell it fast (Knight)
The Efficient Driver's Handbook – Your guide to fuel-efficient driving techniques and car choice (Moss)
Walking the dog – Motorway walks for drivers and dogs (Rees)
Walking the dog in France – Motorway walks for drivers and dogs (Rees)

www.rac.co.uk
www.veloce.co.uk

This publication has been produced on behalf of RAC by Veloce Publishing Ltd. The views and the opinions expressed by the author are entirely his own, and do not necessarily reflect those of RAC.

Although the research for this book was carried out in North America, the findings and implications are international, and all of the outlets and sources mentioned can be accessed via the internet.

First published in September 2012 by Veloce Publishing Limited, Veloce House, Parkway Farm Business Park, Middle Farm Way, Poundbury, Dorchester, Dorset DT1 3AR, England. ISBN: 978-1-845843-79-3 UPC: 6-36847-04379-7

Fax 01305 250479/e-mail info@veloce.co.uk or info@hubbleandhattie.com web www.veloce.co.uk or www.hubbleandhattie.com

Contents

Acknowledgements

As with any book, the author is but an accumulator of the facts and information; acquired knowledge of others, and his own knowledge and experiences: all bound between two covers for the enjoyment and interest of those who read it.

Many highly regarded people in their respective areas of expertise – as well as a host of dedicated organisations – helped with the writing process of this volume. Many thanks to the Canadian Veterinarian Medical Association, the Ontario Veterinarian Medical Association, the Royal Canadian Mounted Police, and particularly veterinarians Doctor Laurel Arvidson, Doctor Cindy Nowle, Doctor Stephen Avery, and Doctor Vince Politi. Without the help of the first two individuals, in both the field of promoting the safety of dogs when travelling in vehicles, and their important input in this book, many more dogs would continue to lose their lives in vehicular accidents.

Safety is of the utmost importance when transporting your dog. (Courtesy Fiona Walker, Camp in a VDub.co.uk)

Special thanks to Rupert Whyte of Historic Car Art/Automotive Fine Art and Vintage Posters, and British artist Roy Putt who allowed us to feature some of his fine paintings. As well, there were many dog and car enthusiasts such as, Ryan, Laura and Rebecca Randall, and their dog, Hazel; Rob Riley of a Toronto-based pet store and his Black Lab, Sam; Wag on the Danforth; Josh Hayter and his dogs, Bauer and Tucker; Roger Murchie and his Duck Tolling Retriever and Lab-cross, Maddie, and Henri and Liz David and their dog, Woodie: all of whom kindly offered us the use of their photographs.

A number of dog lovers and business owners provided information on the many products specifically designed for canine wheeled transportation. This includes the public relations people of Mercedes-Benz, Volvo, Chrysler, Subaru, BMW and Honda who provided corporate information on available options throughout the world. Also, numerous smaller businesses provided help, photos and information, such as Fiona Walker of Camp in a VDub in Britain, and Lorraine Walston of Woodrow Wear (Power Paws),USA.

Very special thanks must also go to Professor Gerald Vise, formerly of the Social Sciences division of York University, Toronto, Canada, for his greatly appreciated knowledge regarding the interaction of human beings and animals. As a York University professor, Vise created his own course entitled "Animals and People," which delved into the attitudes and behaviours of people toward animals.

And thanks also go to Jude Brooks of Hubble & Hattie for her encouragement and support in this project.

And, of course, much love and gratitude to my son, Andrew, photographer and co-collaborator in this book, his patient wife, Catherine, baby Penelope Mort, and rescue dog Riley, who all share in the 'doggy' enthusiasm. Andrew is a graduate of the Ontario College of Art & Design (OCAD) in Toronto. As well as being a freelance photographer, his carefully crafted images have been published in nine other books on various topics over the past three years.

An added appreciation and love to my wife, Sandy, who not only encourages both me and our son, but also acts as preliminary proof reader.

Finally, thanks to perhaps the most important contributors in this publication: the many loving and lovely dogs. Included in the pack was our Golden Retriever, Austin, and Andrew's rescue pooch, Riley, as well as all the other dogs that joyfully helped us illustrate the important points we are trying to make in *Dogs on Wheels*.

British artist Ray Putt has not only captured the sporting character of the car and the driver in this picture, but also that of the dashing four-legged passenger. (Courtesy Roy Putt/Rupert Whyte-Historic Car Art)

5

Foreword

Dogs on Wheels takes an in-depth look at the multitude of considerations and decisions a dog-lover must contend with when taking their dog in a vehicle, be it a trip to the grocery store or on a lengthy family vacation.

In the UK, it is not law that dogs travelling in vehicles must be restrained in a crate or by wearing a harness, though it should be. While no UK statistics exist regarding dog deaths in vehicles, the American Society for the Prevention of Cruelty to Animals (ASPCA) reports that unrestrained pets in a vehicle cause 30,000 accidents a year in the United States. The same source notes that unrestrained dog deaths exceed six thousand per annum.

Although no self-respecting dog-lover would allow their beloved canine to travel like this in an open sports car, both Golden Retriever Austin and Husky-mix Riley look like they would enjoy the experience. (Andrew Mort)

Dogs have enjoyed a long and cordial association in automotive advertising, usually portrayed with a happy couple, or as part of a family, as in this 1952 Studebaker ad. (Author collection)

But, perhaps the most unbelievable statistic is that in the United States a shocking 98 per cent of owners do not restrain their beloved canines when driving, even though 82 per cent of pets travel on holiday with them.

As well as professional transportation and industry advice, and the author's personal insight and research, this book is supported by sound information based on the teaching and lectures of a former York University professor who taught a course on animals in society, as well as information and documentation from expert veterinarians.

This book will strengthen and enhance the unique relationship between you, your dog, and your family, as well as make travelling together safer and more enjoyable. A look at the artistic, whimsical and advertising use of dogs in vehicles over the years adds a light and amusing touch.

For many reasons most dogs love to travel in a car or truck, maybe because they just want to be with us. Dogs make far better backseat drivers than people, and are always great company, which helps the hours and miles roll by much more pleasurably.

Written for dog-lovers everywhere, this book is nevertheless dedicated to the wonderful canines we are so blessed to have in our lives.

Introduction

Travelling with your dog is about so much more than simply plopping your canine companion on the seat of your car. And to better appreciate that sentiment, a closer examination of the dog as a species is required.

There's a huge distinction in the animal world between wild and domestic creatures, and before any wild animal can become domesticated it must go through a lengthy transitional period.

Dogs were the first of the wild animals to be domesticated. There is archeological proof that dogs have lived with humans for over thirty thousand years (cats were domesticated much later).

Wild dogs began associating with humans when attracted to the campfires of early man, and the bones and food that they scavenged there. Man was quick to realise that dogs were useful, and could offer practical help with hunting, as well as guarding,

Well, that's one way to travel! (Andrew Mort)

Did early man seek out the dog or did the dog seek out early man? (Andrew Mort)

Many sociologists believe that the earliest dogs were virtually indistinguishable from wolves. Many of the breeds and crossbreeds we see today seem to back this up.
(Courtesy Volvo Car Corporation)

and a bond soon developed. From these purely pragmatic beginnings grew social relationships and ultimately companionship.

How quickly this transition occurred depended also on the type of dog. Many believe that dogs evolved from wolves or coyotes, or a combination of numerous species of dog-like animals. Sociologists believe that early dogs were virtually indistinguishable from wolves, and much conjecture exists about how the transition from wolf to dog actually occurred. Was it people who turned wolves into dogs or did the animal do it himself?

Dogs have always been intelligent creatures, and maybe they perceived humans as a regular source of food. Evolution over the centuries was, in part, as a result of humans selectively breeding dogs to ensure desirable traits. In fact, part of the definition of a human

being is the ability to control and breed animals: "This manipulation of breeds is typically human, and, as we have discovered, we are very good at it," notes Professor Vise.

Although some societies breed dogs for food, most people today find this repulsive, but as Professor Vise says: "We eat cows, pigs, birds, lambs, deer and sometimes even horses in the western world. There is not a huge difference in eating a dog or a cat. Cultures impact on people and cultures set standards on eating animals."

Over the past few centuries breeding and cross-breeding has created more variety in dogs, and widened canine appeal. In more modern times, as the relationship between man and dog became more and more important, there evolved an aesthetic value to breeding. Dogs have become an extension of ourselves in many ways; the type of dog we own is often regarded in the same way as the type of home or car we possess.

Over the centuries, breeding and crossbreeding has resulted in a wide variety of canines, adding to the dog's appeal. (Andrew Mort)

9

Today, there are literally hundreds and hundreds of breeds of dogs; far more than there are horses, cows or cats. In fact, no other animal embodies such variety in size, colour, intelligence, appearance, and character, apart from people.

Over the last two centuries, our dogs have come to reflect us and our lifestyles more and more. (Andrew Mort)

As well as controlling dog breeding, Professor Vise also points out the social and political relationship that exists between dogs and people.

"In 3200 BC the Egyptians had dogs as pets. There is a possibility those same relationships exist today. But perhaps the relationship between humans and dogs is radically different today or a combination of both. The question is how many different attitudes can people have toward their dogs? Some are over-protective; others not protective enough. Our attitudes toward

Every aspect of a dog's life, environment, and behaviour is controlled by us. (Andrew Mort)

Dogs were the first of the wild animals to be domesticated, and have lived with us for over thirty thousand years. (Andrew Mort)

a dog are often founded simply on the size of the dog or its breed. We react differently to a Great Dane versus a Chihuahua. As well, some breeds are known to be generally more intelligent than others, and far more 'teachable.'

"Teaching them to be with humans is learned behaviour: remember, it is a non-dog world that we humans want them to adapt to. We are creating an interaction between the dog world and the human world. In effect, we are training them in ways to be more human.

"Certain breeds, such as Australian Sheepdogs, Border Collies, Retrievers, etc, are selected to perform specific tasks. In most cases single spoken commands, whistles or hand signals are all that are needed, but this working relationship is also based on a personal relationship that has been developed over time."

Professor Vise adds: "There is a parallel between the dog and human relationship and people and people relationships. Yet, in the case of the dog, we determine what, where, when and how a dog eats, its total environment, and when and how it exercises. We even control where and how he poops. And, as humans we control the dog's behaviour and encourage certain other behaviours. We then try to convince the dog this controlled behaviour is in its best interest as well as ours. Of course, the dog doesn't necessarily see these actions are in its best interest. This also extends to the mode of control in any vehicle."

Many owners today like to humanize their dogs; interestingly enough, most dogs seem to like it! Immie certainly doesn't seem to mind, and looks ready to enjoy the drive (though not on her owner's lap, of course). (Courtesy Hubble & Hattie)

one

Choosing the right vehicle

Which vehicle is best for you and your dog is something that shouldn't be decided on lightly.

The range of available vehicles is impressive, and there are various types to consider. Maybe a Minivan or Van; a small, medium or large two- or four-door saloon; an SUV (four-wheel-drive, Sport Utility Vehicle); a Crossover (a combination of All-Wheel-Drive in a van-like shape); a Pickup; Station Wagon, Convertible – or how about a two-seater sports car? There are advantages and drawbacks with all body styles, making the choice of which one is for you not as obvious as might at first be thought.

In some cases the size of your dog will affect your choice: usable interior space is far more important when transporting a Saint Bernard than a Yorkshire Terrier! And what about the number of dogs that will be travelling at any one time?

Yet another factor to consider is the reason for transporting your dog: pleasure or commercial, such as breeding or showing?

You might think that the obvious choice for those three Collies you have is the biggest SUV, Van, Hatchback or Station Wagon that you can find – but there are other things you should consider.

Access in and out, as well as overall interior size, is important. A family of two or three and a small Yorkie can easily fit into a Mini, Fiat 500, etc, but it's a different matter if the dog is a Dalmatian. Of course, a variant of a small car model such as the Mini Clubman or Countryman can carry larger dogs, but getting in and out of the vehicle could prove difficult. Hatchbacks make life easier in this respect via the use of ramps, although storage of these may prove problematic, depending on design and materials used.

Larger vehicles offer easier access for both people and animals, but there are cost factors, and design is crucial.

Adequate space for your dog and luggage are important factors when travelling in the family vehicle. (Courtesy Volvo Car Corporation)

While testing one of the largest SUVs on the market, our Golden Retriever, Austin, developed a surprise reaction hours after having two injections together during his annual check-up. The reaction was severe and he was definitely in distress, so an emergency trip to the veterinary hospital was in order.

Our large Golden could hardly walk at this point, let alone jump into the SUV. Lifting his back end into the passenger compartment was not an option as the space between the front seat and door post was not large enough. Even more unexpected was that the floor space between the back seat and the front seat was equally narrow, and even when the front seat was pushed forward as far as possible, the space was still too small.

The back side door added to the problem as it would not open a full 90 degrees, and the space between the

Although this small SUV is quite adequate for one child and one dog, it would not accommodate two children and a dog if luggage and other items were also required. (Andrew Mort)

B-post (middle door post) and the seat was far too narrow.

That left just the rear tailgate, but this was simply too high, plus it had a large surrounding lip and a 30cm (12in) wide rear bumper moulding.

The solution was to dig out two tracks of snow about 60cm (2 feet) deep and back the SUV across the lawn to the side porch, so that Austin could walk into the SUV through the open tailgate. (Although a 4X4 vehicle, the snow was too wet and too deep to be sure it wouldn't get stuck.) This was done as quickly as possible, and, fortunately, the coated aspirin recommended by our vet worked even faster, and the crisis was all but over.

Owning more than one dog will also necessitate thoroughly checking a number of items and features before purchase of a vehicle.

15

Unfortunately, there's no magic ratio of interior size versus size of dog(s) and number of people to help you determine which vehicle is big enough. Dogs, people and families come in all shapes and sizes, and apparent interior volume can be deceptive, as numerous large SUVs and Vans are huge on the outside, but have limited usable space inside when it comes to canine and human passengers.

Of course, two dogs need twice the room each, but must also have adequate space to share. With some breeds, such as Chihuahuas, this won't be as much of a problem as two or three Saint Bernards, of course, but don't forget you may also want to carry luggage and other bulky items, as well as other passenger(s). In just over a year your pup will be fully grown, but two children who are small now may find it impossible to travel with two Black Labs five to ten years hence!

As well as the number of people and dogs travelling, the size, age, personality and temperament of all concerned will also directly affect which vehicle you choose, as will the length of the majority of trips you plan on taking together.

Vehicle safety is a major concern of both manufacturer and purchaser, and dog owners should extend the same level of concern to their dog as they do their children. Although airbags save lives, tests have proven they can be harmful to small children, and this will also apply to dogs. So, whatever suggestions or test findings regarding passenger safety exist for your car, apply these also to the transportation of your dog.

How you carry and secure other items in your vehicle can be hazardous to safety. In an accident, loose objects – no matter how heavy – can move or be thrown about. Small objects can become lethal missiles, and larger, heavier items can crush people and pets. Many vehicle manufacturers offer secure screens of metal mesh or vinyl that will safely contain objects in large storage areas, and smaller items can be safely stored in door and seat pockets.

The age of you and your dog may also impact on vehicle choice. At twenty you're much more flexible; able to lift your dog's carrier in and out of that two-door hatch much more easily than

Just as your child should be safely strapped in, so, too, should your dog. (Andrew Mort)

you will do at seventy years of age. And a young dog will leap in and out of your Van without effort, though it could well be a different story when she is older.

Over the last few years some manufacturers, such as Mercedes-Benz, Volvo and others, have offered dog-friendly vehicles with specially-designed options, such as dog guards and screens, to order. Another company which has offered specially-designed vehicles for transporting dogs is Honda, which created a website community in November 2001 for customers who afford their dogs the same consideration when travelling as other members of the family. The website provided information on cafes, restaurants and accommodation where pets were welcome, and encouraged the sharing of ideas from other registered members. It also featured equipment specially designed for dog owners and their dogs.

As a result of this interaction, a model was developed from the ideas suggested by the members of Honda's 'Travel Dog' website community.

When Honda Motor Company introduced an updated version of its 'Vamos' small utility vehicle at the 2003 Tokyo Motor Show, it also announced the 'Vamos Hobio.' This dog-friendly model in the Vamos line-up was developed from information acquired from the website, along with input from specialists, engineers and designers.

The 'Vamos Hobio' was made available as a special limited edition, specifically designed for families with dogs, and called the 'Travel Dog Version.'

In fact, Honda was the first manufacturer to unveil a 'dog' concept car designed to allow owners and their four-legged friend to travel together in comfort, and also supports dogs and their drivers with a range of fun events.

The low, flat floor and wide door openings of Honda's WOW concept vehicle provide easy access for everyone, including canine companions. Note the dog carrier in the rear seat area. (Courtesy Honda)

Features of the model included wipeable door linings for easy removal of dog hair and saliva; specially-designed, wipeable floor mats treated to fight bacteria, odour, and mites; a heater to warm the rear seats efficiently in cold weather; a tote bag for dog walking items; specially-designed stickers, and colour-coded attachment hooks and utility hooks.

Two years later at the 2005 Tokyo Motor Show, Honda unveiled its WOW (Wonderful Open-hearted Wagon) Concept. The WOW was packed with special features, including seats that could be transformed into a crate for your dog, and flexible vents that introduced a stream of fresh air into the cabin. The vehicle's low floor platform allowed for a spacious cabin within a compact body, and a central roof section that could be raised to create a walk-through area for free and easy movement within the cabin.

The interior was clad with wooden flooring reminiscent of a patio, the objective being to make dogs feel more comfortable. The unique interior design was enhanced by the soothing

17

Not what you usually expect to find in a glovebox, but an ideal way to carry small dogs safely, and prevent them from feeling left out. (Courtesy Honda)

interior was four individual seats, though six could be accommodated when the rear seat was slid to the back. The extra, pull-out seat either stowed in the floor, or the seatback and cushion of the extra seat could be detached to form a crate for a larger dog.

The low, flat floor and wide door openings provided easy access for canine companions, the powered, swing-and-slide side doors opening wide to the front and back; the 70/30 per cent, vertically split rear tailgate provided easy access from the back.

look of natural wood, and a state-of-the-art, multi-material instrument panel. Additional innovations included a lid in the instrument panel in front of the passenger seat which opened to reveal a crate for smaller dogs. Mesh at the front and sides assured adequate ventilation, and its position facing the passenger seat made it easy for owner and dog to keep an eye on each other.

Standard configuration of the

Which vehicle's seat doubles up as a crate? A Honda WOW's, of course! (Courtesy Honda)

The powered swing-and-slide doors open wide, and the 70/30 vertically split rear tailgate provides easy access from the back in Honda's 2005 WOW concept vehicle. (Courtesy Honda)

Thanks to the centre walk-through, it was possible to step in at the tailgate and proceed freely all the way to the front of the cabin.

All-in-all, Honda's WOW Concept was full of great ideas to make a dog's life on the road more comfortable, but, alas, did not go into production, although Honda noted some of the concept ideas to offer on other models, whilst others would possibly be modified and incorporated in future models.

A more widely available Honda dog-friendly vehicle was introduced in

Generally available worldwide from 2010 was the Honda Element Dog-Friendly model ...
(Courtesy Honda)

2010. The Honda Element line-up was expanded to include an all-new Dog Friendly™ pet accommodation system. This optional system was specifically designed to improve the travelling safety, comfort and convenience of dogs, *and* their owners.

For example, in daily operation the car kennel kept a pooch properly restrained, so that he could not distract the driver. In the unfortunate event of an accident, the kennel kept the animal contained behind the rear seats, reducing the chance of injury to him and any human occupants.

Some of the Dog Friendly™ equipment enhanced pet comfort by providing a soft floor surface, along with a dedicated fan and spill-resistant water source. Ease of maintenance was improved for owners by an integrated ramp, easy-to-clean surfaces, and a full suite of matching Dog Friendly™ accoutrements.

Other features found in this specially-equipped Honda included a soft-sided cargo area kennel made from seatbelt-grade netting; a cushioned pet bed in the cargo area with an elevated platform; a 12V DC rear ventilation fan; second row seat covers with a dog pattern design (matching the bed fabric); an extendable ramp that stored under the pet bed platform; all-season rubber floor mats with a toy bone pattern, and Dog Friendly™ exterior emblems.

The Dog Friendly™ equipment group had a suggested manufacturer's retail price of £635 ($995).

Although not available worldwide, the introduction of the 2010 Honda Element Dog Friendly™ was an encouraging indication that dog/pet accommodation systems in vehicles were being taken seriously as a major niche market.

Any vehicle manufacturer can launch new, specific 'dog' models or option packages at any time, but often these aren't widely publicized, so it's best to ask your dealer, or check out the manufacturer's website.

Be sure to thoroughly test drive several vehicles you are considering, then shortlist these to two or three, and take your family – including your dog – for another road test. Your car/truck dealer might not like the idea, but that's too bad. Take a blanket for your dog to sit on, and a portable hand-vacuum for any loose hair, but don't take no for an answer. Remember, buying a vehicle is probably the next largest purchase you will make after buying your home.

The following is a list of questions to ask yourself when choosing a vehicle for you and your dog:

- What is the vehicle's ground height?
- Is it designed for easy entry and exit for your dog, and for loading and unloading a carrier?
- How much seating flexibility is there: ie fold-down seating to give more room or improve access?
- Is seating removable when not required?
- Is the seat material designed for wear as well as comfort?
- How many windows are there?
- Are they at a level for seeing out?
- What size are the windows and is there adequate tinting for sunny days?
- Is there adequate heating and air conditioning for the rear seat or compartment areas?
- Where are the ventilation outlets and do all the windows open?
- Does the sunroof have a shade and a variety of optional settings?
- Is rear seating spacious enough for safety harnesses and/or carriers?
- What is the overall ride and comfort level of the vehicle on both paved and rural/country roads?
- How safe is the airbag design when activated?
- Are there proper storage areas for

... which came fully equipped with all your dog could need. (Courtesy Honda)

both heavy and light luggage, parcels, etc, that may otherwise become airborne in an emergency stop or crash situation?

• What is the floor covering and is it easy to clean?

two
Dog travel accessories

Vehicle manufacturers' dog accessories

Despite the fact that so many of us own dogs, only a handful of car and truck manufactures worldwide offer vehicle options or accessories designed specifically for transporting our four-legged friend.

Mercedes-Benz is one that

Honda is one of the few car manufacturers to offer a dog-specific vehicle. (Courtesy Honda)

Mercedes-Benz offers a variety of screens to keep your dog safe and confined while driving. This includes a mesh screen ...
(Courtesy Mercedes-Benz)

... a wire screen to separate the doggie compartment from back and front seat areas ...
(Courtesy Mercedes-Benz)

does, though, as well as a number of accessories for production models to assist with safe travel for your dog. Designed specifically to fit Mercedes-Benz vehicles, these optional extras are also carefully tested to ensure they provide the utmost in safety and security for dogs and people. In addition, they help owners maximize available space for the dog, other passengers, and luggage.

Strong metal dividers are offered for the company's SUVs and Wagons, which allow owners to separate the luggage and dog area, and passenger compartments. Upper and lower dividers are available for some models, along with partition dividers for further division of cargo space: particularly important when it's necessary to separate two dogs travelling together.

... and a multi-split screen for separating two dogs, or a dog and luggage.
(Courtesy Mercedes-Benz)

23

The upper divider can be used separately, but the lower divider can only be used in conjunction with the upper divider. Some Mercedes-Benz vehicles, such as the M-Class and GL vehicles, also offer a more economical solution in the shape of a retractable mesh divider.

To further assist with the transportation of dogs and/or luggage, Mercedes-Benz offers a 'Folding Load Sill Protector,' which not only protects the rear bumper from scratches (as a result of your dog jumping, or being lifted in and out), but also makes it far easier – for older/large dogs in particular – to enter and exit the vehicle safely. The protector simply folds up and stores at the top of the load sill, taking up minimal room but still readily available.

Swedish automaker Volvo is another manufacturer that offers numerous dog accessories for many of its SUV, Wagon, and even car models. In fact, Volvo Cars North America won the Top Pet Safe Vehicle award with the optional pet equipment offered on its 2010 XC60. In the inaugural Pet Safe Vehicle awards in 2008 the winning vehicle was the Volvo XC90.

Quite unique is the dividing luggage compartment in the trunk of the S80 sedan, which Volvo has cleverly designed to keep the luggage on one side and your dog on the other. Although not terribly suitable for large dogs, it is ideal for small and medium hounds with limited access or viewing possible via the folding rear seat, which creates a kennel-like area that can help

For its V70 SUV model Volvo offers this divided luggage compartment which keeps the luggage on one side and your dog on the other. (Courtesy Volvo Car Corporation)

A rather unique option is this divider which turns the S80's trunk into a type of doghouse on wheels. (Courtesy Volvo Car Corporation)

Another Volvo extra is the portable, soft-sided water bowl that can be folded flat and stored out of the way in a seat or door pocket until needed. (Courtesy Volvo Car Corporation)

Volvo offers many canine optional extras including a black neck scarf with dog bone motif for you, and matching fleece blanket and cotton towel for your dog. A rear bumper sill protector is also available. (Courtesy Volvo Car Corporation)

create an environment in which your dog will feel safe and secure.

As well as the more commonly offered dividers specially designed to fit a variety of models, Volvo also has some other, more unique extras, one of which is a foldable water bowl. The black with rubber dog bone logo bowl is fully washable, and has a stay-put rubber base. Due to its fold-flat design it is easily stored, and takes up about as much room as a road map.

Another nice option for those who like to travel in style – and that includes the dog! – is a Volvo-designed neck scarf. Made of 100 per cent cotton, this 50x50cm (20x20in) scarf bears the motto 'Volvo. For Life' on a lime-coloured flag label, the yellow frame containing a pattern of white dog bones.

Other more practical options include a similarly-patterned and coloured 130x170cm, (51x67in) dog blanket of 100 per cent micro-polyester fleece, and a colour-coordinated 30x50 cm (12x20in) towel.

Subaru also offers special optional equipment for dog owners in the shape of easily fitted and maintained floor mats and partitions for most of its Wagon and SUV models.

Subaru offers a variety of dog accessories on numerous models, such as this Tribeca SUV. (Courtesy Subaru)

Shown here is the Chrysler-branded 79x93x5cm (31x36.5x2in) dog bed in the Jeep Grand Cherokee. The cover is easily removable for washing. (Courtesy Chrysler Group)

Chrysler offers an optional, purpose-designed, grey textured, vinyl dog bed to keep your pet comfortable – whilst at the same time protecting the cargo area – in a number of its Dodge, Jeep and Chrysler SUVs and Minivans.

BMW has safety harnesses and dog-proof seat covers in its line-up of vehicles, as well as on various models in its Mini range.

And, on the latest Cadillac SRX, dog owners may choose the optional dividing screen which features an additional strap for attaching the safety harness.

Vehicle manufacturers continue to introduce dog-related travel equipment with new and updated models each year, thoroughly and rigourously tested for use in a particular vehicle.

Dog accessories available worldwide

Many aftermarket travel accessories or fittings are available to help you

BMW is one of the few car manufacturers to offer an optional dog harness for a number of the BMW and Mini models. (Courtesy BMW)

This BMW rear seating area cover is easily installed. The cover extends to the door panels, ensuring that any dirt/debris is contained within it. (Courtesy BMW)

transport your dog safely and in comfort. Most pet suppliers/retailers carry an extensive range of items that vary greatly in price and quality. Thanks to the internet, virtually every product is available worldwide.

Dividers
There are literally dozens of aftermarket metal dividers to fit a variety of vehicles, some of which are safer than others. A metal divider or screen that breaks loose in an accident becomes yet another dangerous object in the interior, so be sure to take your vehicle to the supplier and thoroughly test the fit with your dog present.

Dog socks/boots
For those who want or need to go a step further, available online is Power Paws® in sizes to fit everything from a Chihuahua to a Saint Bernard. Power

Paws® is like a sock with traction pads, which will help keep your dog from sliding around on slick surfaces, and improve his mobility. For traction, it's suggested that the socks are used on the back feet only, although all four paws can be covered.

Further benefits include protecting the interior of your car from scratches and tears in the fabric, and helping to keep it clean. Power Paws® can also help build confidence in an older dog who may not be able to move around so much or so easily.

Dog boots are nothing new, of course, and there are many versions on the market. Although these tend to be more concerned with keeping seats and floors clean, they can also protect your dog's feet from pavement/road debris, as well as hot/cold surfaces. Any sock or boot should fit properly and be easy to remove, yet not so easily that your dog can pull them off. Conversely, if the fit is too snug at the top, this could cut off circulation, so don't buy based on price, but rather design quality and safety features.

There are many different designs of ramp to help your dog get in and out of your vehicle more easily. (Courtesy Honda)

Power Paws® could be the answer if your dog tends to slide around in your vehicle. (Courtesy Woodrow Wear)

This goes for all of the items listed here: some designs are superior to others.

Ramps
Dog ramps vary greatly in design: some will prove too narrow – especially from your dog's point of view – or too slippery or noisy or too steep. The ramp may also be too bulky or heavy to be easily transported.

Inside the vehicle there should be provision to store the ramp; one that is not stored securely may become loose during transit, posing a danger to both four- and two-legged passengers, and even a minor accident could result in major injury in this case.

Dog crates come in a variety of styles and sizes, but regardless of this, all must be properly anchored in the vehicle. (Courtesy Fiona Walker of Camp in a VDub.co.uk)

Speak to your veterinarian, or a specialist supplier, about the type of harness design that's best for your vehicle. (Courtesy Hubble & Hattie)

Crates/harnesses

Once inside the vehicle you have the choice of securing your dog via a special harness that attaches to the regular seatbelts, or in a crate. There are many designs already on the market, with new innovations and safety improvements being introduced each year. Consult your veterinarian for advice, and look for a safety standard on the label or packaging. In the United States pet supply manufacturer Bergan has joined with the ASPCA (American Society for the Prevention of Cruelty to Animals) to support responsible and safe pet travel (see PawsToClick.com).

With rear and side airbags now fitted as standard in many vehicles, the safest tethering spot would be the middle of a rear seat.

There are any number of available dog blankets, liners and hammocks, boasting a variety of comfort and convenience features. Safety is the paramount factor, though, so look for features such as secure, proper fit to prevent your dog sliding around when cornering or braking.

There are also various products specifically for Pickups. A strap on the side of the bed is not a good choice, because although it may prevent your dog actually jumping or falling out, the injuries he may sustain from hitting the side of the vehicle, or, even worse, hanging over the side can easily be life-threatening.

The safest way to travel in a Pickup is to have your dog inside the cab, wearing a purpose-designed dog harness that attaches to the seatbelt, or inside in a secured crate. If there is no alternative to your dog travelling in the Pickup bed, the harness must be a three-point tethered system that ensures the dog stays in the centre of the truck bed. In a minor accident a Pickup topper or canopy will help

If rear seat room is not a concern, a dog hammock provides additional safety measures, while also obviating any possibility of your dog falling off the seat. (Andrew Mort)

prevent your dog from being ejected from the vehicle, but the dog should still be secured. In the case of a severe accident, fiberglass or aluminum toppers often break, come off, or are easily crushed.

Your vet may well be able to offer advice about various crate design attributes or the correct type of tethering for your dog.

Whilst not law in the UK, the Highway Code does note that dogs should be restrained when travelling in vehicles, and insurance companies very often stipulate that animals must be restrained if travelling with you. Some countries within the EU – such as

If your dog is used to wearing a backpack then this is a great way to use up some of that pent-up energy on a brisk walk during a rest break. (Andrew Mort)

Spain – have laws regarding restraining animals in vehicles.

Effects

In today's busy world we seem to need to carry more and more personal items, and your dog will also need a fair few on a trip. Bigger dogs can handle carrying some of these items themselves in special doggie backpacks if out hiking or on long walks. Outward Hound's version comes in various sizes and colours, and the pouches can be filled with practical items such as water bottles and snacks.

Specially-designed water bottles – which have a drinking 'bowl' attached – are available in various styles and designs. This one is called Gulpy®. (Andrew Mort)

three

The dos and don'ts of road travel with your dog

We all tend to think that nothing bad will happen on that quick trip into town, or to the park to walk our dog, but that's why accidents are called that!

Location
Sometimes little dogs and miniatures are carried on the lap of the front seat passenger – or even the driver – and in each case the person will be wearing a seatbelt with a ready-to-deploy airbag in the dashboard. Seatbelts are designed to automatically lock in the event of an accident or emergency stop to prevent passengers from being thrown forward. Should this occur when your dog is on your lap between you and the seatbelt, she will be crushed, possibly to death, and also, in all likelihood, cause you some injury in the process.

If you are holding your dog on your lap when an accident or emergency stop occurs, your natural reaction is

Dog accessories can usually be easily accommodated – no matter how small your vehicle – in interior pockets, glovebox, or even around or in the spare tyre compartment. (Andrew Mort)

to put your arms out to brace yourself, or use them to cover your head. Either

33

way your dog will have absolutely no restraint, and will be thrown around and probably out of the vehicle through the windscreen. Likewise, if your dog is sitting in the rear of your vehicle without restraint, an accident or emergncy stop could propel her forward at great speed, and either into you, the driver, or through the windscreen.

Airbags
Virtually all modern vehicles are fitted with airbags/airbag curtains. Airbags are designed to deploy when a collision occurs at a force equivalent to hitting a barrier at a speed of around 22.5kph (14mph), in an effort to absorb the force of the collision. Although the airbag may save your life, the force and speed (an average of 232kph (144 mph)) at which the bag deploys can actually cause severe injury, particularly if the driver or passenger is not sitting upright and

Harnesses which secure via standard seatbelts are available: this one uses just the seatbelt buckle. (Andrew Mort)

Some harnesses incorporate the seatbelt when it is done up. (Andrew Mort)

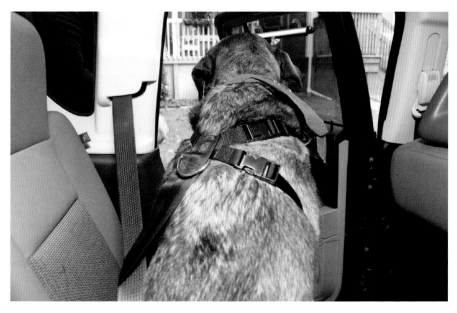

centred in the seat. Consider, then, the likely injuries to your dog as a result of airbag deployment, be that in the front or back seat.

The front seat is not an ideal place for your dog to sit for the same reason that it is not recommended for children under a certain weight and height, as airbags are designed for adult humans. Of course, the consequences will be even worse if your dog is not restrained in any way.

Sometimes dogs are carried in the front passenger footwell, in the belief that this location will afford some protection in an accident. To a degree it will, although the number of leg injuries sustained in accidents is proof that this is not guaranteed. Some vehicles come equipped with knee airbags as a supplement function of a knee bolster in the event of a head-on collision, which is, of course, designed to protect an adult passenger and not a dog on the floor. The same logic applies to side airbags and curtains, plus your dog may even be propelled through the vehicle by an airbag. Read the owner's manual supplied with your vehicle for specific information about the airbags it has.

An unrestrained dog, or one who is allowed to move about within a vehicle, is also a common sight. This is unfortunate, as a dog who is leaping about can easily distract the driver and cause an accident. According to a 2009 report from the American National Highway Traffic Safety Administration, 5474 people were killed and another 448,000 injured in crashes directly related to the driver being distracted. An unknown percentage of those crashes were caused by an unrestrained dog in the vehicle.

It was statistics like these that led to Brtain calling for legislation regarding the need to restrain animals in vehicles. The Highway Code states: 'When in a vehicle make sure that dogs and other animals are suitably restrained so they cannot distract you whilst you are driving, or injure you or themselves if you were to stop quickly. A seatbelt harness, pet carrier, dog cage or dog guard are ways of restraining animals in cars.'

Although failure to observe this recommendation will not necessarily result in prosecution, it may be entered as evidence under the Traffic Act to establish liability.

Even a well-behaved dog that sits quietly without restraint can become a lethal weapon if he is tossed about in a crash.

Pickup beds
The most dangerous way for your dog to travel, however, is in the back of a Pickup. Despite the number of deaths caused by people riding in the back of these, it remains an all-too-common practice. In the United States, for example, it is estimated that, per year, around one thousand injuries, and a hundred and twenty seven deaths of the under-nineteens occur as a result of riding in a Pickup bed. Fitting Camper or Pickup shells offers no additional protection, it seems, and may even cause further injury.

According to the National Children's Center for Rural Agricultural Health and Safety, and the Fatality Analysis Recording System maintained by the National Highway Traffic Safety Administration (NHTSA), in the US, annually between 1994 and 2000, on average sixty three child fatalities of youngsters ranging in age from one to seventeen were associated with travelling in the back of Pickups. Despite these shocking statistics, children are still allowed to ride in the back of Pickups, so it's no real surprise to learn that the number of dogs who do likewise is estimated to be much higher.

If your dog is properly secured via a professionally-designed travel harness to a centre seatbelt restraint, or well secured in a crate, her chances of avoiding major injury in the event of an accident or emergency stop are greatly increased.

Windows

Most vehicles today are equipped with air conditioning, but we all still love to travel with the windows down; so does your dog. Dogs are commonly seen enjoying the ride with their heads stuck out the window, but this is a very dangerous practice, as apart from the possibility of a head or neck injury, there's also a risk of contracting eye and ear infections. Conjunctivitis is a common ailment that can occur due to wind irritation to the eye, for example.

In addition to having their heads out the window, many dogs will also have their feet up on the window ledge, which puts them at risk of ejection in the case of a sudden stop. Dogs can also be crushed, potentially fatally, by a window that is accidentally or suddenly raised by a child or forgetful owner.

Doctor Laurel Arvidson recalls: "I saw a Greyhound that was killed when a toddler hit the window button and crushed the dog's larynx: the dog had been riding with his head out of the window. Despite heroic efforts and placement of a tracheotomy tube, the dog was brain dead and died shortly afterward. Electric windows move up and down very quickly. I'm sure that there have been dogs ejected when a window they were leaning on suddenly disappeared because someone, or the dog, pushed the power-down button."

A good general rule of thumb is to apply the same safety considersations to your dog as you would a child.

Cold

If travelling to cold or snowy areas, ensure your dog does not suffer from frostbite and/or hypothermia. While short periods in the cold should not be a problem, be aware that there are circumstances where even this can prove dangerous, especially if your dog is old and not in the best of health. Check with your vet before you go.

To avoid your dog suffering heat stress or heatstroke when travelling, never, ever leave her in the car on her own – even if all of the windows are open and the car is in the shade.

In 2011 Harvey Locke, President of the BVA, said: "The British Veterinary Association is proud to be part of the 'Don't Cook Your Dog' campaign. It's a simple but tragic fact that dogs die in hot cars, and we need to get this message out to every single dog owner. Dogs should never be left in cars by themselves. Even when the day is just warm, not hot, it can quickly become very hot inside a vehicle. Leaving windows open and a bowl of water is simply not enough. Dogs perspire primarily through their tongues and paw pads, so can't cool down quickly enough to cope with the rising heat in a car."

Your dog can also suffer heat stress whilst the vehicle is moving, if the temperature should rise rapidly. Despite what may be considered adequate ventilation by us, an older, overweight, or short-nosed dog is more prone to heat stress. Dogs literally cook in hot cars – a horrible, excruciatingly painful death. Make sure it doesn't happen to yours.

Dos

Start early
If you plan to take your dog with you in your vehicle on a regular basis, start

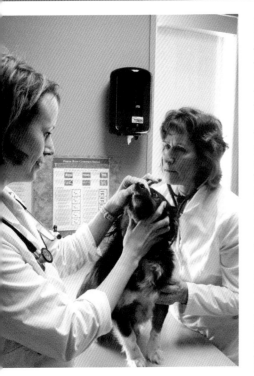

It's a good idea to have your dog checked over by your vet before setting off on holiday or a lengthy trip, as he or she can advise you about your dog's current health status, and any issues that may be relevant to where you are travelling. (Courtesy L Arvidson)

Familiarisation

It helps immensely if you begin crate training at home as well as when travelling, and, if you prefer to use a harness, begin getting her used to wearing it around the house before trying it in the car.

Ideally, you should expose your dog to the sound of airplanes, other cars/ motors, and other loud, sudden noises during this socialisation period, as this will make for more relaxed travelling, as well as a calmer dog when walking, playing, etc. You can buy recordings of these noises, as well as recordings intended to soothe your dog when travelling.

One ten month old rescue puppy my family adopted was very well behaved, but absolutely terrified of cars and trucks: he was so paranoid he gave every vehicle a very wide berth indeed. Eventually, with a lot of reassurance, he was able to ride in a vehicle, but for years he was sick every time, no matter how long it was since his last meal. We later discovered that if lay down on the seat so that he couldn't see out, he was better, but if he sat up and looked out the window it was time to reach for the towel!

Feeding/exercise

That brings us to the point that you should feed your dog well in advance of setting off in your vehicle, or plan on feeding him when you stop for the day. A dog who suffers from motion sickness should not be fed for at least eight hours before travelling. Your vet can give advice about safe medications to control nausea or anxiety if further measures are needed. You should also exercise your dog in the usual way before leaving, to allow him to empty his bladder and bowels.

It's important that your dog has access to fresh water during journeys,

the trips early in her life. If your dog has grown up used to travelling in a vehicle, it will be a much more comfortable experience for all concerned, and a building block in her socialisation process.

Vets recommend that a 'positive vehicle experience' should occur at an early age in the crucial socialisation period of eight to twelve weeks, during which time frequent, short rides on an empty stomach are encouraged as nausea can be an unpleasant experience that your dog may come to associate with the car.

Exercise your dog as you usually would before starting your journey. (Andrew Mort)

particularly if they are long ones. Ordinary bowls will allow water to spill out: those with lids designed specifically for travel are an alternative, although water can still end up on the floor or seat in a moving vehicle.

If you are driving in warm weather your dog will pant more in an effort to stay cool, increasing his evaporation rate. Ensure you make frequent stops to offer your dog fresh water so that he is comfortable and not at risk of dehydration.

Security

Ensure that your dog always wears an identity tag on his collar with at least two contact numbers on it (not his name, though, as this could assist would-be dog thieves). It's strongly recommended

Dehydration can be life-threatening to your dog, so ensure you carry plenty of fresh, bottled water. (Andrew Mort)

that you also have him microchipped. In the event that he should become lost, there's every chance you can be reunited.

Health/medication

If you are travelling away from home for a period of time, always carry your dog's vaccination record and any health certificates as a precautionary measure.

If travelling abroad, note that different rules and regulations apply in different countries, so thoroughly check these out before departure to prevent delays or being refused entry. All medications that your dog may need should be purchased ahead of time in sufficient supplies.

Another health consideration is if your dog requires a monthly heartworm preventative, other non-core vaccine protection, or flea and tick protection (based on where you are travelling). It's good practice to take your dog to the vet before setting off on a lengthy trip or holiday: your vet knows your dog and has all her records, and can identify any health changes or concerns.

A first aid kit should be a standard item in any vehicle, and also ones for dogs. It's possible to buy CDs that teach you doggie first aid, as well as books (see *Further reading*).

Restraint system

If your dog sleeps in a crate at night, he should not have a problem travelling in this way; he may even prefer this to sitting on a seat. Size is a factor, obviously, as the dog must be able to travel comfortably, whatever the journey length. As a rule, the crate should be roomy enough for your dog to stand up, turn around and lie down in comfortably. The crate should be secured to the floor or wall of your vehicle to prevent it sliding around or being thrown about in the event of an accident.

The alternative would be a barrier that separates the seating area from the crate, although your dog would still need to be secured to prevent him from being thrown about.

Numerous restraint systems are available on the market, often differing greatly in design. The weight and size of your dog will be a deciding factor in which you choose and, again, your vet can probably advise you about what type would be most appropriate for your dog.

Control

Have your dog's lead readily to hand for rest breaks, and in the event of an emergency. Travelling with two leads is not a bad idea as this allows you to keep one in the passenger glovebox and another in a door or seat pocket for convenience.

Some dogs are apt to bolt when let out of a crate or the door is opened, so ensure you attach the lead before opening the door, as a dog jumping out of a vehicle runs the risk of being hit by traffic or causing an accident. Don't keep a lead on your dog when actually travelling, though, as this can become tangled or caught on something, which can also prove dangerous.

Essentials

Depending on your destination, taking extra bottled water for your dog may be something to consider: if you have concerns regarding the local water and the effects it may have on your health, these concerns apply equally to your dog.

Make sure you have an ample supply of bags to pick up after your dog.

Comfort and interaction

If your dog is properly restrained in the back seat, consider asking one of your passengers to sit with her. A dog is a very sociable animal, and may feel rather isolated alone in the back; a loving scratch behind the ear from time to time will reassure your faithful, four-legged friend.

If you usually talk to your dog, be sure to include her in your conversation when travelling, mentioning her name to let her know you are talking to her. If conversation lapses, one of your passengers could perhaps read a story to the rest of you (and your dog) to help the hours pass.

Crack a side window or the sunroof to allow fresh air into the vehicle. Although we may only notice the strongest smells that permeate the car, your dog – with some two hundred and twenty-five million olfactory receptors – will register and enjoy them all. Whilst we are highly visual creatures, a dog views the world through her nose.

Dogs who are used to a warm home, and who have travelled to somewhere cold in a warm vehicle, are in danger of getting frostbite and/or hypothermia, so gradually acclimatise him to avoid these dangers. Shorthaired, very young/old, small or sick/older dogs – or a dog whose coat is wet – are particularly vulnerable. Puppies less than a month old can suffer from hypothermia even at room temperature if away from their mother/littermates.

Comfortable, safe and enjoyable travel with your dog should be as automatic as fastening your seatbelt, and sitting back to enjoy the ride.

Reading helps pass the time on a long trip. If your child and your dog share the backseat, then sharing a book, too, can be fun for them both. (Andrew Mort)

four

A dog's psyche when travelling: the joys, fears, and phobias

It's mostly assumed that all dogs love to travel in cars with their owners, but we should remember that a dog was never meant to ride in or on anything with wheels.

From a dog's point of view, lying down on the back seat of a car, where he probably can't see what's happening, can be very strange indeed: he senses and feels movement, noise and bumps, yet is not moving himself!

A dog is territorial by nature, and may assume that the entire back seat is his domain, in which case an enclosed area or crate may be preferable for all concerned, and this will also provide a feeling of security for him.

Not all dogs are created equal in size, intelligence and disposition, of course, and this must also be considered. Certain breeds are better able to interact well socially with other dogs, people and children, and a change in environment, making them better able to cope with car journeys

Remember that your dog has no idea were she will be going when she jumps in the car. Is this a trip to the park for a romp ... or a visit to the vet ... she doesn't know but looks forward to the ride anyway! (Andrew Mort)

with you and possibly other passengers.

Professor Vise stresses: "As owners we have to adapt our dog up to a certain point. Is that point shorter for us and further for them? Sitting in the back

Are we off to the woods, the beach, or grandma's house ...? (Andrew Mort)

seat of a vehicle is an adaptation to the human world."

When it comes to choosing our dog, we probably take into account her breed, size, intelligence and personality, but if you want your dog to travel with you often then this, too, should be a factor in your choice.

When it comes to a dog's personality, this can vary greatly from breed to breed, and even within the same breed.

"Some dogs are also more fragile or more anxious than others, while other dogs are more robust," notes Professor Vise. "For whatever the reason, even members of the same breed can differ. Therefore, adapting to a new human

environment – in this instance a vehicle – can create anxiety. It is much like us adapting to a non-human world, such as a diver in deep ocean waters would do. This new situation creates anxiety; sometimes a lot, sometimes not. Every dog is different, and this also needs to be considered."

The home you have made for your dog, and how you are with her, also impacts on how she will react to a new mobile environment. Some people spend a lot of time with their dog, taking them everywhere that they go, whilst others are away most of the day (which is not recommended as dogs suffer from loneliness and boredom in this situation). Some dogs become child

A dog is usually happiest being included in whatever his family is doing. (Andrew Mort)

There's more to going for a drive with your dog then simply placing him on the backseat. (Andrew Mort)

As Professor Vise points out: "Every dog is different, which should be taken into account when deciding on the vehicle and type of harnessing you will use."
(Courtesy Fiona Walker, Camp in a VDub.co.uk)

substitutes; others are trained only to be guard or work dogs.

Professor Vise also notes: "Owners have to ask themselves how much these dogs need to adapt. They must provide the dog with food, water, a collar and lead, etc. All of these forms of human adaptations, aimed at control of

Professor Gerald Vise, Cheryl, and their Beagle, Patrick, about to set off for a safe ride in the family Volvo. (Author collection)

the dog, should be considered. A puppy has no socialisation or adaptation other than being with its mother, but we remove it from its only known environment and the first thing we do is bring it home in a vehicle."

Obviously, this can be a time of great anxiety for many young dogs.

Dogs are very adaptable and trainable in a wide range of situations, but, whatever kind of relationship you have with your dog, does this change when you travel with him in your car?

For example: "Is a guard dog still a guard dog when being transported, or just a dog in the backs eat? This location in a vehicle also influences a person's behaviour, as well as the dog's," says Professor Vise.

An off-duty guard dog has nothing to guard while travelling on the back seat of a vehicle, and may well become anxious as a result. Consider whether he might feel more at ease in his own, more private space, such as a crate, which could well be more familiar to him.

Do dogs suffer from claustrophobia or agoraphobia? Before you set off on that 3-hour journey, it would be a good idea to try out some shorter trips first to check for signs of distress or anxiety in your dog.

five

Veterinary advice for travelling with your dog

Introduction

Laurel Arvidson and Cindy Nowle are associate veterinarians of the Lacombe Veterinary Centre, working largely in a rural community. These two dedicated vets were responsible for initiating a local poster campaign in conjunction with the RCMP Police Dog Services Training Centre aimed at educating the public about potential dangerous situations resulting from travelling with unrestrained pets in a vehicle.

Laurel Arvidson recalls: "A few years ago I saw a dog that had caused a rollover and multi-car pile-up on a highway. It was a young lab, loose in the front seat, who got really excited by a big truck driving past. She started jumping and barking, and then hit the gearshift, knocking the car out of gear. The owner panicked and ended up rolling the car. The dog was ejected from the car and then, despite injury, ran back out onto the highway and caused

Veterinarian Cindy Nowle and her dogs, Enzo the Chihuahua, and Reno the Aussie, enjoy some time together. (Courtesy L Arvidson)

another accident. A trucker stopped and was finally able to catch the dog. The dog's owner had to be airlifted to hospital. The dog was pretty lucky in

Veterinarian Laurel Arvidson taking a relaxing walk in the woods with her dog, Norman. (Courtesy L Arvidson)

A dog who is not properly restrained within a vehicle runs the very real risk of falling or being thrown out, with possibly fatal consequences. (Author collection)

the end as it had only moderate nerve damage to a forelimb, which eventually resolved. It could have been much, much worse had she been hit by a car going 110kph (65mph).

"It also goes without saying that that dog could have caused serious injury or fatalities to the passengers in the other vehicles involved. That trucker, in spite of his good intentions, could have also been seriously injured trying to catch the dog – which was racing from one side of the highway to the other for quite some time – had he been hit by a car. Our poster campaign idea came shortly after this when we realized that there was nothing in existence at the time which we could use to let people know about safe travel."

She continues: "This campaign, then, stemmed from our frustration at seeing animals which had been involved in automobile and truck accidents come into the veterinary centre with preventable injuries. We have seen dogs after they have gone flying into the windscreen or had their foot caught in the steering wheel after the driver has braked suddenly. We want people to remember that a big, loose dog is like having a person in the back seat without a seatbelt on! Every year there are a significant number of injuries or fatalities with drivers and front seat passengers who are hit by an unrestrained person in the back seat. A dog – just like a person – can also be a lethal projectile in the case of a collision."

As well as trying to warn owners about the dangers of the all-too-common practice of carrying unrestrained small dogs on laps, and big dogs with their head out of the window, a central thrust of the campaign was directed at dog owners with Pickups.

"I have seen more shredded foot pads and foot fractures than I can even

Approved and tested enclosures are available from some car manufacturers, such as this example by Subaru. (Andrew Mort)

remember, but one in particular does come to mind. A middle-aged Husky cross that was ejected from the truck box at about 75kph (45mph) landed on her feet, and proceeded to leave most of her foot pads on the highway. It was several months of intensive care and medication before that dog could walk normally again. It's very sad to see dogs that have been seriously hurt after falling out of a Pickup, or ejected into traffic and then run over. The outcome is often euthanasia."

Arvidson also recalls: "We once had a client who 'tried to teach his dog a lesson' on how to ride in the back of his truck. The owner was annoyed that the dog kept putting his front feet up on the toolbox he had at the front of the box (I'm guessing that the dog was trying, like many of them do, to look over the top of the cab). So, the owner started swerving in order to teach the dog not to go up there. What he ended up doing was ejecting his black lab from the truck bed and he fractured his femur on impact."

In any vehicle a dog must be securely and safely tethered.

"Some owners mistakenly tether their dogs in the back of their trucks with a single long line. If the dog leaves the truck bed for any reason the end result is it being dragged along behind the truck or hanged by its own collar," warns Arvidson.

The highly successful campaign eventually went province-wide in Canada, and Doctors Arvidson and Nowle received communications awards from the Alberta Veterinary Medical Association in 2010 in recognition of their public service. Since that time the posters have gone country-wide, which had been the hope of the two doctors.

Cindy Nowle adds: "Another goal of the campaign was to just get people involved in making policy and enforcement laws about dog safety in vehicles."

This awareness of dog safety in vehicles soon led to new local by-laws, and is now being included in provincial legislation in Canada. In America some

US states have already made pet restraints mandatory in vehicles, while in Britain awareness is growing, and possible legislation being discussed.

Diet

Ensure no sudden change in diet before taking your dog in a vehicle, as this can cause vomiting and/or diarrhoea, say Arvidson and Nowle. They also say: "Frequent small portions of the dog's regular diet will minimize motion sickness. It is also okay to give a slow, reward-type treat while in transit: for example, a Kong™ filled with kibble or a frozen canned food to eat while in the crate, as these will last longer. Chew items will also alleviate boredom if your pet is not prone to nausea."

Health

There are three major health concerns to be aware of when transporting your dog in a vehicle.

Motion sickness
This is a problem for many canines, as the movement of the vehicle causes a dog to become nauseated, which usually results in vomiting. This may also occur if the dog is not restrained in any way whilst the vehicle is moving.

One of the first signs of motion sickness in a dog is usually excessive salivation or drooling, and repeated licking of the lips. Sometimes simply stopping the vehicle and taking your dog for a short walk, or having a play period will help – at least for a while.

Not feeding your dog for eight hours prior to departure will also help, as will ensuring adequate ventilation in the vehicle at all times.

If motion sickness occurs at the puppy stage, often, frequent short trips on an empty stomach could help the

problem, and the dog should eventually grow out of this habit. With many dogs, the less they are able to move around in the vehicle the better. Motion sickness is often made worse by sudden changes in position and/or location within the vehicle (try turning around to face the rear when going up and down a couple of hills).

If all else fails, your vet can prescribe safe, anti-emetic medication.

Heat stress/heatstroke
A leading cause of canine death in vehicles, unbelievably, dogs are *still* left alone in cars. Even on a day that we might consider only warm, the temperature inside a car can rapidly rise and endanger the life of your dog.

For example, 24 degrees C (75 degrees F) outside can be over 37 degrees C (100 degrees F) in a car, and this rise can occur quite rapidly, even if the vehicle is parked in the shade.

Doctors Arvidson and Nowle confirm: "A greenhouse effect can happen very quickly. If your dog is suffering from heat stress or heatstroke, seek veterinary help without delay. To help on the way, fan your dog, and lay cool, wet cloths on her to reduce body temperature."

Frostbite/hypothermia
Frostbite and/or hypothermia is equally dangerous to your dog's health, and can result in death.

Frostbite
Frostbite is caused by extreme, cold temperatures and results in the skin tissue – usually the extremities – freezing and dying, while hypothermia occurs when body temperature becomes too low as a result of cold, shock, after anaesthesia, and in newborn puppies.

Frostbite can affect ear tips, tail, paws, testicles, and nipples. Initial signs are areas of numbness, coldness and/ or pallor which will later become red, swollen and possibly painful. Severe frostbite is indicated by blisters forming, and areas of the skin dying off (white, numb body tissue). In less severe cases some of the coat hair may fall out, regrowing white.

Hypothermia

Hypothermia may not always be present with frostbite. The first symptom will be shivering, as the body tries to warm himself (small dogs are at a greater risk than large dogs because they have less surface area and lower body weight). Should the shivering begin to abate, this is because the dog's mechanism for maintaining his body temperature is failing. This slowing down or stopping is not a good sign, therefore, as it means that the blood vessels are beginning to dilate, and body temperature is rapidly dropping, combined with many other symptoms:

- Excessive whining and shivering
- Anxious attitude; seeking shelter/ protection
- Blood vessels dilating
- Low body temperature (groin area is cold to touch)
- Mental sluggishness, slow movement and dullness
- Drop in pulse rate
- Drop in blood pressure
- Shallow and slow breathing
- Dog is unresponsive
- Unconscious state develops
- Death occurs eventually

In the case of both frostbite and hypothermia, it is vital that you get your dog to a vet without delay.

Comfort/mental state

Take care to ensure that your dog is calm and comfortable during any trips

In the case of either frostbite or hypothermia, seek veterinary help immediately. Here, Dr Stephen Avery of the Leslieville Animal Hospital examines Riley. (Andrew Mort)

he takes with you. Even before you set off, he will have sensed that something is going on, and the change of routine, preparation for the trip, or simply being in the vehicle with you will cause him to feel excited and, in some cases, anxious.

If your dog becomes overly-stressed, it may occur to you to use one of the drugs on the market that claim to alleviate this problem, yet veterinary recommendation is to only use these if absolutely necessary.

Make sure that your dog travels in comfort and safety. (Courtesy Honda)

Doctors Arvidson and Nowle stress: "Avoid sedatives as these can cause dangerous fluctuations in blood pressure. A safer option includes antihistamines like Gravol and Benadryl which will cause a mild drowsiness and ease travel anxiety.

"Always discuss the dosage of these medications with your vet, and try out the antihistamine at home in a controlled and supervised setting to see how your dog responds to it before using it for your trip.

"For some dogs homeopathic products such as Rescue Remedy™ or those containing trypic casein may be helpful."

As to how often you should stop for rest breaks when traveling in a vehicle with your dog, Arvidson and Nowle have

this to say: "It depends on the animal. Ideally, frequent stops for a high-energy-type dog and less often for low-energy types, but keep your pet's needs in mind: health issues, fresh water, regular meals, an opportunity to empty bladder and bowel, and to stretch his legs to prevent stiffness are all things which will make your dog's journey more comfortable and pleasurable."

Safety

Like many veterinary associations around the world the Canadian Veterinary Medical Association (CVMA) has taken a strong position with regard to dogs riding in cars. And, in many cases, in Canada it is or soon will be illegal to transport any animal – and particularly a pet – that is not secured to

Ensure both your child and your dog are safely buckled up. (Andrew Mort)

ensure the safety of all occupants of the vehicle.

The CVMA states: "Dogs are sometimes transported unsecured in the bed of a Pickup or flatbed truck, placing them at increased risk of injury. Dogs that ride in the open back of Pickups or other open motor vehicles are in danger of losing their balance, even with steady driving, and especially in the event of sudden stops and turns. Injuries may occur as a result of falling or being thrown from the vehicle. Motorists or pedestrians may be injured in ensuing traffic accidents.

"Some jurisdictions have enacted legislation prohibiting the transportation of dogs outside the passenger compartment of a vehicle unless the animal(s) is secured in a firmly anchored kennel or other prescribed animal restraint device."

Happily, veterinary associations around the world have set up similar programmes, and echo the CVMA's sentiments. It's a fact that in North America many semi-rural practices see at least six to ten dogs a year which have been injured as a result of not being restrained in a vehicle.

"In addition to the dogs we see immediately after an accident, we also hear a lot of stories about more minor accidents and injuries from our clients who have been just as careless, but luckier. Potential injuries include head trauma, foot pad trauma and fractures." say Arvidson and Nowle.

Dogs can appear unscathed from an accident, but internal trauma may include bleeding and/or organ damage. Corneal injuries have also been reported in pets who have had an airbag deploy in their face. Some fractures are easy to spot, although pelvic, rib or small bone fractures are not nearly as obvious. Shock is also common and can be extremely serious and even life-threatening because it can lead to complete failure of the circulatory system. Initial signs of shock/injury can include:

• Changed behaviour
• A fast, palpitating hearbeat and quick, shallow breathing
• Asymmetrical pupils
• Lameness
• Pain

• Cold to the touch
• Apathy/listlessness/lethargy
• Disinterest in food and water
• A longer capillary refill time (CRT)/pale mucous membranes (inside of eyelids, gums, muzzle, anus, vulval vestibule)

To test your dog's CRT, with one finger press on the gum for one second and then release. There are many small blood vessels, called capillaries, in the gums, and, when an area of the gum is pressed, blood is forced out of these capillaries. When the pressure is released, the blood should almost immediately refill the capillaries. The time between removing the finger and the return of colour to the gum is called the capillary refill time.

six

Travel breaks: the how, where, and why

Although we are usually keen to arrive at our destination, long hours on the road are not advisable for man nor beast. Rest breaks are important for physical and mental health, and there are many nice places where you can stop to allow you and your dog to take a much-needed break. It's important on especially long journeys that the breaks are regular; maybe every one to two hours as a guide.

Our journeys tend to be driven on the fastest roads in order that we get to our destination more quickly, but this usually means that we miss out on the numerous small towns and villages which offer a much safer, quieter, and restful place to stop away from the constant stream of traffic.

Just like you, your dog will be ready for a break from travelling after a couple of hours ...
(Andrew Mort)

... and will welcome the opportunity to get out and stretch his legs. (Andrew Mort)

Here, you can usually find dog-friendly parks and quiet pavements for some exercise and stress-relief. Of course, you and your dog may also be in need of food, drink and bathroom facilities, so choose a spot that can provide these. Be sure to observe any rules or regulations that apply to your dog during your break, and ensure you pick up after him.

After a spell in the car, you may find that your dog becomes excited when you stop, glad of the chance to get out, stretch her legs, and have a good sniff around, so always attach her lead before letting her out of the vehicle. A reflective lead and collar are safer at night.

To make a rest break as effective as possible, try and walk for 15 minutes or so with your dog – off-lead if possible to allow a good sniff around and a chance to toilet. (Andrew Mort)

One of the benefits of finding somewhere to take a rest break well away from traffic is that your dog can safely run off-lead for a while. Maybe there's time for a game or two. If playing ball is a favourite, consider taking along a Chuck®: it's less of a strain on you but still a lot of fun for your dog. (Andrew Mort)

Always have your dog under control as even the most obedient and well-behaved canine can be startled by unusual things and occurrences, such as large vehicles, other animals, children, and any number of unusual noises. And check that she is wearing something with all of her contact details just in case you somehow get separated.

If you feel that your dog is overheating, offer plenty of fresh, cool drinking water. Gently bathing her ears and feet with cool water may also help.

57

Even older dogs like Black Lab Sam get a sense of puppy-like excitement when it's time to take a break on a long car trip. (Andrew Mort)

Put leads on your dogs before letting them out of your vehicle. (Andrew Mort)

Dogs are social animals. If you can find somewhere that your dog can play off-lead with lots of other dogs, all the better. What a great break! (Andrew Mort)

Just as we can, your dog can also become stiff and tired after a long journey, so ensure your rest breaks allow for time to walk a little, and ease any aches and pain.

Some fresh air, exercise and relaxation outside the confines of your vehicle every hour or two will help everyone feel better prepared for the rest of the journey.

By leaving the main road you can very often find somewhere really nice where you and your dog can relax and enjoy a break. (Andrew Mort)

Many towns and villages have parks away from traffic for off-lead fun – but remember to pick up after your dog. (Andrew Mort)

seven

Having fun with your dog when travelling

Children today have it very easy when it comes to things to do on a long journey: they can watch films, play electronic games, listen to their own music as loudly as they want, thanks to earphones, or do all sorts of things with the latest, high tech smartphones. Looking out of the window and I-spy just don't come into it!

Dogs, on the other hand, usually have nothing more interesting to do than listen, smell, watch, and sleep.

There is some wisdom in the old adage 'Let sleeping dogs lie,' and if this is what your dog is happy to do, then that's fine. But if he's looking a little lost

As well as exercise and fun, rest breaks should also include some quiet time with your dog. Quietly petting and talking with your dog will provide the attention she needs, and prepare her to go quietly back into the car to resume your journey. It will also relax you and relieve any stress you may be feeling.
(Andrew Mort)

or lonely, perhaps some attention from you or someone else in the car can comfort and reassure him.

No two dogs are alike, of course, and this also goes for what sort of attention and contact they prefer. Will a gentle scratch behind the ear of your snoozing dog send him into a blissful state – or give him quite a start?

It's not necessary to rough-house with your dog to keep him amused; save that for one of your rest breaks. Apart from reading out loud, singing and talking to your dog, and the usual petting, scratching and cuddles, there are many other things that will help while away the time.

For example, a massage could be just the thing to relax your dog. Rubbing favourite scratch spots is always usually welcome, especially if you wear a glove or sock over your hand to give a different sensation to usual.

Simple games for quick amusement include gently pushing a sock ball over to your dog's nose, which she will usually nudge back to you. Peek-a-boo

with your hands or a coat can also be fun, and the old childish game of pat-a-cake can keep you both amused.

Try gently placing your hand on top of your dog's paw, and I bet you'll be surprised by how quickly he reverses the move.

These are simple games designed to break the monotony of the journey, and include your dog in what's going in. They're also a great way to prepare and energise your dog prior to a rest break.

Then again, maybe your dog would like to watch an old dog film with you in the back of the car? Many family vans and SUVs have optional DVD players or computer plug-ins, and there are lots of dog flicks, including even classic animated canine adventures such as Disney's *101 Dalmations*, and *Lady and the Tramp*.

When giving your dog treats, how about using a puzzle toy or a Kong™ so that the experience lasts longer? Or introduce a bit of fun, perhaps, by seeing if your dog can guess which hand the treat is in?

If possible, interact with your dog during your journey. (Andrew Mort)

eight

Dogs on two wheels ... and other forms of road transport

Motorcycles and scooters

Carriers

Motorcycles are a popular mode of transport with many, but carrying your dog on two wheels is not as safe as it is in a four-wheeled vehicle, for obvious reasons. Still, people want to travel with their dog on two wheels, and, in most cases, the dog does, too.

When this happens, often – as with cars, Vans and Pickups – little or no consideration has been given to the animal's safety in the event of an accident. A dog who has been trained to sit or stand on the seat behind their owner on a scooter or motorcycle might look cute, and is clearly enjoying himself, but the dangers are blindingly apparent.

Often, miniature, small, and, in some cases, even medium-sized dogs have been seen travelling on motorcycles and scooters in a specifically-designed saddle bag,

chest- or backpack. Some small dogs of less than 7.2kg (16lb) in weight can be trained to sit on special padded seats that fit over the motorcycle fuel tank and partially onto the seat, though

Woody in his owner's vintage American Woody station wagon. (Courtesy Henri and Liz David)

There are various ways that you can safely transport you and your dog on a motorcycle. A harness like the one Immie has on here is fine for a car, but not suitable for use on a motorcycle, though Immie still wears hers, even when only posing. (Courtesy Hubble & Hattie)

there must still be adequate room on the seat for the rider. Safety rings are provided with these seats with which to secure the dog, and should be used at all times.

Another widely available option for tiny dogs is a specially-designed, helmet-shaped/sized container that fastens securely on the rear seat or luggage rack of the motorcycle.

Bear in mind, though, that many of these methods of transporting your dog on a motorcycle are not recommended for extended travel on the road.

Sidecars
A sidecar is another possibility for allowing motorcycle and dog enthusiasts to combine their passions. An air conditioned, enclosed sidecar provides more than adequate protection, and the dog can be securely attached to the seatbelt in the sidecar via a harness, just as in a car. It's even possible for the owner to talk to her canine companion through a stereo/intercom-type system.

An open-air sidecar can pose the same potential health problems as those of a dog sticking his head out the window of a car or in the bed of a Pickup, although it is possible to buy canine goggles and helmet, as well as other fitted 'leathers' which should help with this if your dog is happy to wear these.

Trailers

Still another option is a dog trailer designed to be towed behind a motorcycle. From the outside these often look like miniature horseboxes, and inside they are lined with insulation and foam padding on the floor, with removable carpeting.

Other features can include vents and sliding windows with screens for ventilation, various styles of rear door, and numerous other comfort features. A partition can be used for storage or

another dog. A motorcycle pet trailer/ carrier can be custom-ordered to accommodate your breed of dog or dogs.

Similar carriers are available for bicycles, including lightweight trailers, as well as the traditional front and rear baskets, which are usually padded and lined, and come with restraint straps.

Other modes of transport

Camper vans, motorhomes and caravans are all great vehicles in which to travel and holiday, but just because they are homes on wheels, it doesn't mean that they don't have safety concerns.

The advent of seatbelts dates back to the early 1950s, but because they were optional rather than mandatory,

Camper vans such as this VDub (Volkswagen) are ideal for family vacations and travelling, but remember that the same safety issues apply here as with all other vehicles. (Courtesy Fiona Walker of Camp in a VDub.co.uk)

This tiny, 1966 Fiat 500-based Autobianchi van is perfect for easy entry and exit, and has both a seatbelt in the front and grille divider for fastening Austin's harness, the author's Golden Retriever. (Author collection)

not many vehicles of pre-late 1960s vintage were fitted with this life-saving equipment, and even now, owners of old vehicles do not retrofit non-original equipment in many cases.

It is not illegal to drive a car without seatbelts if it was manufactured before belts became standard or mandatory fixtures. Even so, there are many ways to secure a crate or harness in an old vehicle to enable you and your dog to safely enjoy a sunny day at a car show, autojumble, drive or cruise event

without drilling holes or permanently compromising originality. For example, straps and tie-downs can be attached to seat frames or other fixed items in the interior to secure a crate, and harnesses simply attach to standard seatbelts.

Remember, too, that in an accident, items within your motorhome or camper can get thrown about inside, just as an unrestrained dog can be, so be sure that everything is firmly secured before setting off.

Dogs traveling with their owners in 18-wheeler trucks is a tradition in some countries, and often inspired by the truck manufacturers themselves. (Andrew Mort)

et MACK's newest

... a truck-about-town

The cab-forward

MB DIESEL

Built for the brutal stop-and-go of city traffic—a new Mack diesel in the cab-forward class. A truck-about-town. The all-around delivery vehicle everyone's been looking for from Mack—The MB.

Use the MB with a stake body, van, tank or semi-trailer. Haul most anything ... you'll deliver it more profitably with a Mack MB truck or tractor.

nine
Dogs on wheels in art and advertising

Dogs have been travelling with their owners since the invention of the horseless carriage around the turn of the century, and evidence of this can be found in literature, film, paintings, advertising, brochures, books, and photographs, and even sculptures depicting people riding in cars with their beloved dog or dogs alongside them.

Adverts

The use of dogs in car advertisements dates back to the earliest drawings, though most often the dog was usually seen barking at and chasing the new-fangled horseless carriages that were

This 1930s press photograph says as much about the couple as it does about the car in terms of style. The dog adds a humanitarian touch, as well as an endorsement of their apparently chic lifestyle. (Courtesy Daimler-Benz)

These dogs in the high-priced 1950 American Chrysler 'Woody' Town and Country advertisement emphasise a sporty lifestyle. (Author collection)

In 1930s photographs, films and advertising, the dog was most often portrayed working and assisting his owner, as in this case, out hunting. (Author collection)

The DeLuxe Ford V-8 Station Wagon

Sporty, luxury car advertisements, such as this 1950s BMW 503 Cabriolet, often pictured a dog. (Author collection)

Surprisingly, few car advertisements focussed on the family, but one of the few exceptions is this one for the 1960s Morris Minor 1000 Traveller. (Author collection)

Purchasers of two-seater sports cars more often than not did not have children, so the marketing people felt they should have a dog. The new 1962 Triumph TR4 could easily accommodate a medium-sized dog on the back shelf behind the bucket seats, though not, it must be said, very safely ... (Author collection)

Size really DOES matter, as these large dogs in the hatch area of a 1960s 875cc (53ci) Singer Chamois brochure illustrate.
(Author collection)

responsible for so much noise and dust.

It wasn't until later, in advertisements of the 1920s and early 1930s, that dogs were positively pictured as part of the scene, standing or sitting alongside the automobile being advertised, very often in front of a grand house. The dogs shown were usually noble-looking breeds such as the Borzois, Poodle, or Wolfhound, with only the best-dressed and most fashionable people riding in a fine automobile or pictured welcoming friends to their stately home.

Afghans, Setters and Spaniels – with their sleek bodies and wavy coats – were used to accentuate the curvaceous lines of sporty cars and convertibles, and add style to fashionable, high-priced sedans and town cars, whilst Labradors were thought to epitomize a 'sporting' lifestyle or be an essential element of the 'perfect' family.

By the 1950s the Beagle, Dalmatian, German Shepherd and Black Lab were popular breeds in advertising

and brochures. However, as new trends and fashions in society and lifestyle evolved over the decades, the breeds of dog used in automotive advertising changed, too, and today Sheepdogs, Labrador Retrievers and Golden Retrievers have seen an increase in popularity as 'family dogs,' and are used more and more in advertising. Some dogs were also considered a symbol of strength, and truck manufacturers used them in adverts to emphasize the size and might of their products.

The term 'family dog' was commonly used by the 1930s, although our canine friend had yet to achieve the exalted and somewhat pampered status he holds today. A dog was often taken

France's Renault also used the dog as a symbol of stylish, free-spirited sporty character, as demonstrated by this mid-70s brochure for the Renault 15TL. (Author collection)

Hmmm ... a one-dog car, apparently! (Author collection)

Mack's Bulldog epitomized power and toughness, and became the symbol of this famous American trucking company. The sculptured bulldog mascot is considered art today. (Andrew Mort)

on to work and perform certain tasks, from herding and hunting to protection and guarding.

Film

Dogs have always been popular in motion pictures, and some – such as Lassie and Rin-Tin-Tin – have achieved star status in their own right.

American silent movies of the 1920s, such as *The Little Rascals,* and later 1930s series films like *Topper* and others, influenced our view of and feelings for the family dog. The American film series, *The Thin Man*, based on the books by Dashiell Hammett, changed the dog's status in the eyes of millions of dog owners forever. Highly popular stars William Powell and Myrna Loy played Nick and Nora Charles, who quickly became two of the most stylish and popular American socialite on-screen couples of the 1930s and early '40s. Ex-detective Nick and wealthy heiress Nora solved crimes in their spare time in six highly successful MGM Hollywood films. Riding around in open Packards and Cadillac models with their feisty Wire-Haired Fox Terrier, Asta, the glamorous couple solved often grisly crimes with humour and great panache.

The 1984 hit film *Gremlins* (Warner Brothers) had an early sequence with animal-lover Billy Peltzer (played by Zach Galligan) trying to take his dog, Barney, to work with him, but his old VW Beetle just wouldn't start. As Billy sighs, Barney whimpers in sympathy: obviously a car dog!

In *Turner and Hooch* (Touchstone), the dog, Hooch, is eventually seen as a positive influence in the police detective's (Turner's) life, although early scenes depict every dog-owner's nightmare. Detective Scott Turner (Tom Hanks) is forced to adopt the

Brockway borrowed a leaf from the Mack book and chose the Husky as its logo. When it introduced an even more powerful truck it used two Husky dogs as hood ornaments and in its ads. (Andrew Mort)

dog of a dead man to help him find his murderer. Inside the car, in exasperation the detective yells at the continually slobbering French Mastiff "Don't eat the car! Not the car! Oh, what am I yelling at you for? You're a dog!" Despite sometimes dreadful behaviour, Hooch goes everywhere with his newly self-adopted owner.

By this point in our four-legged friend's establishment in the position of beloved family pet, filmgoers regarded Hooch's behaviour as amusing rather than wrong: a strong social statement in itself. A similar storyline was used in *K-9* (Universal Pictures), starring James Belushi and the clever German Shepherd, Jerry Lee.

Since the 1990s and into the new century, dogs in films have generally featured as important members of the family, holding almost the same status

Roy Putt studied drawing and graphic design at Bournemouth College of Art, but ended up in a successful rock band, becoming a professional musician before he decided to concentrate on a career in motoring art. (Courtesy Roy Putt/ Rupert Whyte-Historic Car Art)

as children or a spouse – and in some cases higher!

A favourite film for dog lovers is *My Dog Skip* (Warner Bros) by Willie Morris, about his first dog, Skipper. In the film not only does Skip ride in the family car he's also seen driving it!

Art

Prominent painters of automotive art and sculpture have used dogs in their creations, and more recent automotive art has featured canines enjoying themselves in motor vehicles.

A good example of this is the work of British painter Roy Putt, one of numerous contemporary artists who have added a dog to their vintage car renderings.

Roy Putt has become a regular exhibitor at such prestigious automotive events as the Goodwood Festival of Speed, Silverstone Classic, Le Mans Classic, and Race Retro. His work has also been exhibited at The National Motor Museum, Beaulieu, and at race courses such as Donington, Gaydon, and Brooklands.

Many of Roy's award-winning paintings feature a dog in a car, adding life, charm and character and, in some cases, a sense of speed, too as the wind lifts and ruffles the animal's coat.

Dogs in vehicles can often be found in sculpture or pottery in more recent times, and for over a hundred years, photographers have included dogs in pictures of families in their cars.

Today, the dog is included in photos as a fully paid-up member of the family, and very often has the distinction of posing solo for his or her own photo gallery. It's not unsual to find framed photos of beloved dogs on mantelpieces, walls, and office desks – not to mention as computer and mobile phone screensavers.

As well as paintings, advertisements, brochures and books, dogs are often featured in sculpture and pottery. (Andrew Mort)

Books

Dogs in vehicles have also enjoyed a long history in literature, and perhaps the most read stories worldwide are those of the late James Alfred Wight, OBE, FRCVS (3 October 1916-23 February 1995), also known as Alf Wight, but more familiar to millions as English vet James Herriot.

His popular books – *All Things Bright and Beautiful, All Creatures Great and Small*, etc – make many references to the companionship he and his dog(s) enjoyed driving around the Dales to attend the many animals that required his care.

In children's literature, families having travelling adventures with their dog feature widely: Tintin and Snowy by Herge, Gumdrop and Horace by Val Brio, Cadillac by Charles Temple, and numerous others.

It's really not surprising that dogs should feature in so many areas of our lives, as they always give so much to us, whether or not they're in the car!

Another example of one of the many fine paintings by award-winning British artist Roy Putt, featuring a sporty car and equally sporty-looking dog. (Courtesy Roy Putt/Rupert Whyte-Historic Car Art)

The tales of well-loved English vet James Harriot brought joy to millions of dog lovers, including the author. (Author collection)

ten

Appendix

Alphabetical list of useful contacts

American Society for the Prevention of
Cruelty to Animals (ASPCA)
www.aspca.org

Bergan Pet Products
www.berganexperience.com

BMW UK
www.bmw.co.uk

British Small Animal Veterinary
Association (BSAVM)
www.bsava.com

British Veterinary Association (BVA)
www.bva.co.uk

Canadian Veterinary Medical
Association CVMA
www.canadianveterinarians.net

Chrysler UK
www.chrysler.co.uk

Department for Environment Food and
Rural Affairs (Defra)
http://www.defra.gov.uk

Ford UK
www.ford.co.uk

General Motors UK
www.vauxhall.co.uk

Honda UK
www.honda.co.uk

Mercedes-Benz UK
www.mercedes-benz.co.uk

Paws To Click
www.pawstoclick.com

Putt, Roy
www.historiccarart.net

Royal Society the Prevention of Cruelty
to Animals
http://www.rspca.org.uk

Volvo, UK
www.volvocars.com/uk

Woodrow Wear, USA
www.woodrowwear.com

Further reading

*Complete Dog Massage Manual –
Gentle Dog Care* ISBN 9781845843229
Hubble & Hattie (www.hubbleandhattie.
com)

*Dog-friendly breaks in Britain (Special
Places to Stay)* ISBN 1906136602
Alastair Sawday

*Dog Games: stimulating play to
entertain your dog and you*
ISBN 9781845843328
Hubble & Hattie

*Emergency first aid for dogs – at home
& away* ISBN 9781845843861
Hubble & Hattie

Pet Friendly Places to Stay 2012 ISBN
074957142X AA Publishing

*Walking the dog – French motorway
walks for drivers and dogs*
ISBN 9781845844295
Hubble & Hattie

*Walking the dog – Motorway walks for
drivers and dogs*
ISBN 9781845841027
Hubble & Hattie

78

Index